TONY ABBOTT

★ BOOK 1 ★

WADE AND THE SCORPION'S CLAW

KATHERINE TEGEN BOOKS
An Imprint of HarperCollins Publishers

Katherine Tegen Books is an imprint of HarperCollins Publishers.

The Copernicus Archives #1: Wade and the Scorpion's Claw
Text copyright © 2014 by HarperCollins Publishers
Illustrations copyright © 2014 by Bill Perkins
www.harpercollinschildrens.com

Library of Congress Cataloging-in-Publication Data
Abbott, Tony, date
  Wade and the scorpion's claw / by Tony Abbott. — First edition.
    pages cm. — (The Copernicus archives ; # 1)
  ISBN 978-0-06-231472-7 (paperback)
  [1. Adventure and adventurers—Fiction. 2. Voyages and travels—
Fiction. 3. Antiquities—Fiction. 4. Secret societies—Fiction.]
I. Perkins, Bill (Illustrator), illustrator. II. Title.
PZ7.A1587Wad 2014   2014010026
[Fic]—dc23   CIP
                                                                  AC

Typography by Michelle Gengaro-Kokmen
14 15 16 17 18   OPM   10 9 8 7 6 5 4 3 2 1
❖
First Edition

CHAPTER ONE

Somewhere over the Pacific Ocean
Sunday, March 16
3:51 a.m.

It was only a dream—a dumb, exhaustion-fueled dream.

But knowing me, the way I hold on to stuff forever, I don't think I'll ever forget it. I'll probably always remember it as *the dream*.

To begin with, my name is Wade Kaplan. I'm thirteen years old and kind of a math geek. I live in Austin, Texas, though I haven't been there for a very long week. At the exact moment I was having *the dream*, my family and I were squished on the first of three endless flights from the tiny island of Guam in the South Pacific to New York City.

We were on our way to meet someone who could

help us understand what had happened yesterday—the day my stepmom, Sara Kaplan, was kidnapped.

More on that later.

To go back a bit, Sara married my astrophysicist dad, Roald Kaplan, three years ago, and her son, Darrell, became my new stepbrother and absolute best friend. While I was in the middle of *the dream*, Darrell was crammed into the row right next to me. Dad sat three seats beyond him, across the aisle. Sandwiched between were Lily Kaplan, my cousin on my dad's side, and Becca Moore, her best friend.

They were the last people I saw before I closed my eyes somewhere between Guam and Hawaii and my dumb dreaming brain took over.

I was in a cave. No, scratch that. I was in *the* cave— the cave where we had found the first of the twelve relics of the Copernicus Legacy.

Yep, that's what I said: the Copernicus Legacy.

You see, five hundred years ago, in the early sixteenth century, the astronomer Nicolaus Copernicus went on a secret journey and uncovered the remains of a large astronomical instrument.

This ancient device, a kind of oversize astrolabe— with seats in it—contained twelve amazing objects that gave the machine its unbelievable power.

Power to travel.

In time.

That's right. The past, the future, the whole spectrum of time from the beginning to, well, I guess, the end of it.

Anyway, Copernicus's mortal enemy, a guy named Albrecht von Hohenzollern, learned about the astrolabe. Albrecht was the Grand Master of the superpowerful, incredibly secret, and seriously evil Knights of the Teutonic Order of Ancient Prussia.

Copernicus knew that if Albrecht and his Order got hold of the time machine, they'd use it to rip the fabric of our universe to shreds.

So Copernicus did the only thing he could do.

He took the astrolabe apart and asked twelve friends around the world to hide and protect its twelve powerful relics. These men and women were called Guardians.

Okay, back to the dream.

Every detail of the cave's stony walls had been downloaded onto my brain's hard drive—the rough limestone, streaked with yellow and red, the constellations painted on every surface all the way up the tapering walls to the opening at the top, the blue handprint that pointed the way to the first relic, and, above all, the incredible silence of the stone. The cave seemed nothing less than a kind of temple from another world.

So I was standing in the center of the cave,

when—*whoosh*—there he was, with a cape and a velvet hat, and a sword longer than your arm.

Nicolaus Copernicus, the revolutionary astronomer who proved that the earth revolved around the sun, and not the other way around. He was standing not ten feet away from me next to his awesome machine—a large sphere of iron and brass and bronze, in the center of which sat a pair of tufted seats.

To be honest, the dream Copernicus looked a lot like my dad, with a beard and glasses. That was weird enough. But everyone else was in the cave, too, and they were all sad, like someone had just died.

Lily was sobbing like a baby. "Oh, Wade," she said. "Oh, Wade!"

Like Lily, Darrell was crying but also shaking his head and stomping around like an angry bull. (That's actually kind of what he's been doing ever since he heard about his mother, and I don't really blame him.) Finally I saw Becca, lying on the floor of the cave, not moving, her arms over her chest. I probably dreamed that because Becca was wounded in the cave in real life. But here she looked, you know, the opposite of alive.

"Becca?" No answer. "What's going on? Somebody tell me!"

Nobody told me anything. Then Copernicus-Dad came over to me.

"Vela," he said, his face dark under his hat. "I need it now."

Just so you know: Vela is the relic of the astrolabe that we found in the cave.

For the last five centuries, followers of the original Guardians have kept the relics safe, using codes, clues, riddles, and mysteries that would twist your brain into a pretzel.

Until last week.

Galina Krause, the Teutonic Order's freaky-beautiful new leader, ordered the murder of the communications chief of the modern Guardians, an old man named Heinrich Vogel.

To me, he was Uncle Henry, my father's college teacher and friend.

Don't ask me how we did it, but following a number of clues Uncle Henry had left for us, we found the first relic before Galina did—a small blue stone called Vela— in that cave in Guam.

At that moment, we became Guardians of the Copernicus Legacy. I guess one part of that means having crazy dreams like this one. Another part is that members of your family get taken away from you.

"Wade, please . . ."

I handed Vela to Copernicus-Dad. He attached the triangular blue stone to the time machine.

"You see," he said. "All things are possible. . . ."

I knew it was my own mind saying that. I mean, it was my dream, right? But it felt like Copernicus-Dad was telling me, too. "Cool," I said.

Suddenly, the big wheels of the time machine began to turn, and the cave became hazy around me.

"All things are possible, Wade," he said. "Except one . . ."

"Wait. What?" I said.

Then *she* was there—Galina Krause with her nasty crossbow, the one she used to wound Becca. "Where is the twelfth relic?" she demanded.

I looked around frantically, but now I was alone. Darrell, Lily, Becca, even Copernicus-Dad had vanished. Galina closed in, her crossbow aimed dead at me. I tried to yell, but the oxygen in the cave was sucked away. I couldn't breathe. The cave went pitch-black and as silent as a tomb, until Galina spoke.

"Die, Wade Kaplan, die!"

I heard the click of the trigger as the arrow left the bow.

I heard the whoosh in the air . . .

. . . and felt the arrow's razor tip enter my chest. . . .

CHAPTER TWO

"**A**hhhh!"

I jumped like a jack-in-the-box. About an inch off my seat. My seat belt was fastened tight and dragged me down hard.

"Ahh . . . mmmph!"

Darrell had his hand clamped over my mouth. "Dude, really? Screaming in a jet? The pilot's gonna ask you to step outside."

I pushed his hand away. I was soaked with sweat, my head was throbbing, my heart was thundering, and *everyone* was staring. I'd just had . . . *the dream*.

"Sorry. Nightmare." I coughed.

Darrell grunted. "Join the club. Except it's no dream. We left Guam on Sunday, right? But guess what? It's

Saturday again. We just crossed something called the international date line, which turns today into the day before today. So instead of yesterday, Mom was kidnapped two days ago."

He slammed his fist on the poor armrest. "Great, huh? We're going backward."

"Darrell . . ." I wanted to tell him that the international date line didn't actually mean what he said, but what really struck me was that I'd dreamed about a time machine at the exact moment we—sort of—went back in time. Before my dream, it was Sunday. Now it was Saturday. A coincidence?

Except I don't believe in coincidence anymore.

The plane descended into Honolulu, and it was good to feel the jolt of the wheels touching the ground. Before anyone else could, I grabbed Becca's bag for her. After Galina had grazed her with the arrow in the cave, we helped Becca in little ways. Her wound was a day old—or two, if you were Darrell—and wasn't close to healing. I shivered, remembering her lying on the cave floor in my dream. At the very least, Becca needed to see a doctor so we'd know she was really okay.

There was a rush of movement and new air and crammed bodies as we stumbled through the Jetway and entered the terminal, but the moment I set foot in the arrival gate area, I tensed up.

"Do you guys feel that?" I whispered. "Somebody's eyes are on us."

Becca glanced around. "I do. I'm pretty sure no one followed us from Guam, but someone's watching us now."

"They're probably hiding inside recycling bins," Lily muttered. "Or disguised as young moms with strollers. The Order is too smart to be seen, and they have to be, because otherwise everybody would know about them, but no one knows about them except us, of course, which goes without saying, but there you go, I said it anyway."

That was a perfect Lily kind of sentence. I was getting to like how she got so much in before she ran out of breath and had to stop.

"Kids, look," Dad said, slowing and facing us. "You're right to be cautious, but sometimes people are just people, you know? It doesn't help to see trouble where it isn't. We have enough to think about without imagining enemies."

Dad might have been right—he usually is—and by "enough to think about" he probably meant Sara. But ever since we attended Uncle Henry's funeral in Berlin, we'd been squarely on the Order's radar. Later, after we'd overheard Galina Krause say, "Bring her to me. Only *she* can help us now," we knew that her ugly goons had kidnapped Sara.

What that meant was simple.

Finding the relics and rescuing Sara had become the same quest.

Looking as exhausted as I've ever seen him, Dad said, "We have a good bit of time in Honolulu before our flight to San Francisco. I know we're all hungry, but I want to find a walk-in clinic where someone can take a look at Becca's arm. Then we'll get a bite to eat."

"A clinic would be great," she said, smiling. "Thanks."

It was a quick hike past restaurants, souvenir shops, and newsstands to a little clinic, where an intern cleaned and changed Becca's bandage. After he was done, and Becca gave us the thumbs-up, we headed slowly in the direction of our next departure gate, taking a round-about route. I mean, we *knew* the Order would know where we were sooner or later, but we wanted to make it as difficult as possible for them. We started in the opposite direction, doubled back, entered shops and left at different times from different exits. It was probably overkill, but all part of our new way of doing things.

Luckily, there was no rush. Our flight to San Francisco was still several hours away.

I should mention that we've learned to travel light. Pretty much all I keep in my backpack are a change of jeans, two shirts, underwear and socks, an extra pair of sneakers, and a baseball cap. In a leather envelope, I carry the celestial map that Uncle Henry gave me on my seventh birthday. It was a major clue in starting us on the search for the relics.

Oh, and I also have two sixteenth-century dueling daggers.

Not your normal luggage, I know. One of the daggers belonged to Copernicus, the other to the explorer Ferdinand Magellan, who turned out to be Vela's first Guardian. I sort of argued with my dad that because he had Vela hidden in his bag, it was smart for someone else to hide the daggers. Besides, the security-evading holster the Guardian Carlo Nuovenuto had given me in Italy was so techie, I'd successfully brought both blades through several security checkpoints. Dad agreed.

Security had become a major priority, for obvious reasons.

Carlo had also given us a new cell phone, but we were pretty sure it had been hacked in Guam, so Dad stopped at a kiosk and bought us three new ones, another part of his plan to throw off the Order. He gave a bottom-of-the-line one to Darrell, kept one for himself, and gave a high-end smartphone to Lily.

"I feel like a spy," she said, admiring its features. "I guess we make only essential calls and searches?"

"Exactly," my dad said. "No way are these a gift. We need to take our situation seriously. We'll keep only

11

each others' numbers, and every few days, we'll get new phones. It'll be expensive, but safer. It's just one way to stay ahead of the Order."

Near our gate I saw a place called the Diamond Head Pineapple Snack Hut, and my stomach grumbled. Because of the time difference between Guam and Honolulu, not to mention the date line, it was by now late afternoon local time, but our internal clocks were so messed up that we pretty much ate whatever we wanted whenever we could. Pancakes and pizza, grilled cheese and fried eggs, sodas and hot chocolate.

While Darrell and Dad went to order, the rest of us sank into our chairs and spread our junk on the table. Since I'd been writing down clues and riddles in my dad's college notebook, it had sort of become mine, and it was becoming as valuable as anything we had.

After I scanned the tables around us—everyone sitting at them seemed like passengers as tired and grumpy as we were—I leafed through my latest notes while Lily searched for an outlet. She is an awesome online searcher, which is why she got the best phone. She can take a blobby mess—sometimes all we can come up with—and create a search term that will—*boom*—get the exact answer we need.

Looking both ways, Becca dropped her hand into her bag. "Guys," she whispered like a conspirator, "I want to show you what I found in the diary."

A ripple of excitement shot through me with the speed of Galina's arrow. As good as my notebook is, and as awesome a searcher as Lily is, there is nothing like the book Becca slid onto the table and quickly covered with her arm.

The secret diary of Nicolaus Copernicus.

CHAPTER THREE

The Copernicus diary's actual title is *The Day Book of Nicolaus Copernicus: His Secret Voyages in Earth and Heaven*.

The old book was started in 1514 by the astronomer's assistant, a thirteen-year-old boy named Hans Novak. It ended about ten years later, penned by Copernicus himself.

Because Becca is a total language expert, having learned Spanish, Italian, German, and bits and pieces of other languages from her parents and grandparents, she's been translating the entries into a red Moleskine notebook.

"On our flight here, I found eleven passages at the

end of the diary," she told Lily and me. "All of them are coded. We tracked Vela a different way because it was the first relic, but I think each of these eleven passages might be about one of the other original Guardians and his or her relic, but I need a key to decode them. Actually, I need eleven different keys, because they all seem to be coded differently."

"Do you think the key words are somewhere in the diary?" I asked.

Becca shook her head. "Not the key words, but there's this."

She gently slid her finger down a single page at the end of the diary. Unlike most other pages, its outside edge wasn't ragged, but straight.

"That looks different," said Lily. "Was it cut or something to make the edge straight?"

"I thought so, too," Becca said. "But no." She ran her finger between that page and the facing page, deep into the gutter of the book. There, with a slender fingernail, she peeled the page back, revealing that the straight edge was in fact a fold. The page's flap was inscribed with a large square of letters.

```
w z y x u t s r q p o n m l k i h g f e d c b a
z y x u t s r q p o n m l k i h g f e d c b a w
y x u t s r q p o n m l k i h g f e d c b a w z
x u t s r q p o n m l k i h g f e d c b a w z y
u t s r q p o n m l k i h g f e d c b a w z y x
t s r q p o n m l k i h g f e d c b a w z y x u
s r q p o n m l k i h g f e d c b a w z y x u t
r q p o n m l k i h g f e d c b a w z y x u t s
q p o n m l k i h g f e d c b a w z y x u t s r
p o n m l k i h g f e d c b a w z y x u t s r q
o n m l k i h g f e d c b a w z y x u t s r q p
n m l k i h g f e d c b a w z y x u t s r q p o
m l k i h g f e d c b a w z y x u t s r q p o n
l k i h g f e d c b a w z y x u t s r q p o n m
k i h g f e d c b a w z y x u t s r q p o n m l
i h g f e d c b a w z y x u t s r q p o n m l k
h g f e d c b a w z y x u t s r q p o n m l k i
g f e d c b a w z y x u t s r q p o n m l k i h
f e d c b a w z y x u t s r q p o n m l k i h g
e d c b a w z y x u t s r q p o n m l k i h g f
d c b a w z y x u t s r q p o n m l k i h g f e
c b a w z y x u t s r q p o n m l k i h g f e d
b a w z y x u t s r q p o n m l k i h g f e d c
a w z y x u t s r q p o n m l k i h g f e d c b
```

"It's a cipher, but I don't know how it works yet," Becca said.

"I'll tell you!" Lily bounced up, tugged her phone from the charger, and immediately started tapping on its screen.

"How do you even know what to search for?" I asked.

Lily snorted. "Because while your brain is going 'huh?' mine is going 'aha!'"

I glanced over my shoulder. Darrell and Dad were loading up their trays.

"It's called a *tabula recta*," said Lily. "It's a 'letter square,' created by a cryptological guy named Trithemius in the sixteenth century." She flipped her phone around and widened an image with a swipe of her fingers. It was almost identical to the hand-inked square Becca had found in the diary.

"You did it again, Lily," I said.

She gave a little bow. "Trithemius's square includes twenty-four cipher alphabets, so each time you code a letter—say *L*, for Lily—you give it a different letter. It's nearly impossible to figure out without the key word. Trithemius was all about improving codes."

Dad and Darrell wove through the food court with two trays full of food. I trotted over to help and noticed that Darrell's eyes were red. I knew right away that he and my dad had had a time-out.

"Until we get to New York, we're not going to make much headway," Dad was saying.

"I get it," said Darrell. "I just wish it were all happening faster. I keep thinking of Mom in some dark place with no food—"

17

"You can't go there, Darrell," Dad said. "You'll only twist yourself up in knots, and we don't know anything real yet. Look, let's eat; then we'll call Terence Ackroyd, all of us. Get the latest. Okay?"

"Good. Yeah. Let's do that." Darrell settled his tray in the middle of our table. While he stuffed a pineapple spear into his mouth, Becca showed him and Dad the letter square and one of the passages.

Darrell snorted. "Beefy kahillik buffwuzz ifgabood?"

"I think you added some letters there, but either way, without the key word, it means nothing," Becca said.

"Unless you're an ifgabood," he said.

Aside from the funny nonwords, Darrell wasn't into it. He calls ciphers "word math," which is actually a clever way of describing them. Darrell doesn't plod through stuff. He's an improviser. Tennis. Guitar solos. He has to jump from one thing to another, one thought to another, one move to another, just to compete. All that moving sometimes makes him hard to follow and jumpy.

Sometimes it makes him plain brilliant.

Dad perused the diary. "Eleven passages. One for each of the other relics . . ."

"I think so," Becca said, twisting her lips as she often did when she was deep into translating. "We have to find the key words, but I don't think they'll come from

18

the diary. I think they're out there. In the world. We just have to be smart enough to find them."

"Good thing we've got such a smarty-pants like you in our gang," said Lily, winking at her.

Becca smiled. "Thanks, but you better save the compliments, at least for now. Breaking the code is going to be super challenging."

The rest of our brunch-lunch-dinner passed pretty much in silence. I could tell from Darrell's dark looks that he was going where my dad had told him not to go. Thinking about his mother trapped in a cold dark place with no light, no heat, no food . . . now I was doing it.

Finally, Dad keyed in Terence Ackroyd's number, and we all went quiet. He was about to put it on speaker when it apparently went to voice mail. He hung up without leaving a message and looked at his watch. "It's nighttime there. Maybe he's out. He'll call back." He stood abruptly. He scanned the concourse in both directions, looking for what, I wasn't sure. Teutonic Knights? I glanced around, too. No one seemed overly suspicious. Which, of course, made me more suspicious.

"Okay, team, good lunch," he said, trying to smile but not quite making it. "We need to keep moving."

I got what he was doing. Dad had done this my

entire life—taking all the danger and scary stuff into himself so that no one else would worry or feel bad or be afraid.

If only it were that easy.

CHAPTER FOUR

After we spent almost three more tiring hours zig-zagging among the airport's hundreds of shops, being tricky but not really seeing anyone we could identify as being from the Order, we headed to the gate to rest and wait. The Honolulu-to–San Francisco flight was still a little over an hour and a half away, but I was surprised to find that the gate had already begun to fill with passengers from Hong Kong, whose earlier flight was joining ours. We found five seats together and settled in, then I went to look out the window.

It was evening now and the sky had darkened enough for the first stars to be visible, even over the brightly lit airstrips.

"Where math and magic join up, right?" whispered

Darrell, sidling up to me. "What Uncle Henry said about the sky?"

I turned to him. "You *do* listen when I tell you stuff."

"Sure," he said. "Just not all the time."

Where mathematics and magic become one was the way Uncle Henry had once described the sky to me. It was a magical place of stars and constellations and planets, always in motion, an area where science and mysticism wove into each other. Except now the sky had become something even more. It had become our way of life.

"You should try to sleep," I told him as we headed back to the others. "We all should. We have another hour at least before we can even board."

"I can't sleep," Darrell said, slumping into a seat next to Becca, stretching out, then hunching over, ready to bolt up. "Sleep is for other people. I hate waiting here. It's dead time."

"Have you tried humming a lullaby inside your head?" Lily asked, probably hoping a joke might distract him from his mother's disappearance.

He groaned. He wasn't taking the bait.

Sara is Darrell's actual mom, so of course he was in worse shape than the rest of us, probably even Dad. Not knowing the fate of someone you love is crushing. I love Sara, too. We all do. But for Darrell it's definitely the hardest. She's his mother, the one who fed him and read to him and nagged him and held his hand when he had nightmares. It was kind of amazing he wasn't even more of a wreck than he was.

"If I fall asleep," Darrell said, staring at his hands as if wondering what they were for, "will it mean I'm not thinking about Mom?"

"That's so not possible," I said, and then added, "but I get it. No one's going to be right until Sara's back."

Becca grabbed my sleeve. "Him. On our left."

I think I actually shuddered when she said *him* and was instantly on edge. I turned my head slowly and saw a tall man in a long black leather coat striding into our gate. He carried no luggage, and his hands were driven deep into his coat pockets. He paused, pulled one hand out to glance at his phone, and then pocketed it.

"He's German," Lily whispered. "You can tell by his shoes."

I believed her. Lily knew fashion backward and forward and usually got it right about stuff like that.

The man couldn't have been more than ten years older than my dad, but his hair was as white as snow and cropped very short. I could see his face was weathered, as if he'd spent a lot of time outside.

"Plus, he's *totally* overdressed for Hawaii," Lily added. "Which makes him too suspicious not to be evil."

"Lily," said Dad softly, eyeing the tall man. "Don't go overboard."

She frowned. "Okay, but just in case, my code name for him is Leathercoat."

"He's with the Order," Darrell said, raising his eyes to the man.

Becca shivered and twisted away in her seat. "At least he can't do anything to us out here in the open. . . ."

"I agree with Darrell," I said. "Everyone's with the Order—"

A baby laughed suddenly.

"The baby, too?" Lily asked with a smirk.

"Probably in training," I said.

The baby's laugh was full-throated, and so was his mother's. The reason was a middle-aged man, one of the passengers joining us from the Hong Kong flight. He knelt in front of the stroller, making faces, then tipped over and balanced on one hand, his long black hair dangling to the floor. The baby practically exploded in laughter. Finally, the man jumped to his feet and took a low bow.

Several people clapped, including Lily. "I used to be able to do stuff like that," she said. "Not since sixth grade, though. I'm rusty."

"I never knew you were in the circus," Darrell teased her despite himself. Joking around was his way of covering up his feelings.

"I was," she said flatly. "It's where I first saw your clown act."

He grumbled a laugh, which was as good as he could do. I looked around. Leathercoat had wandered away, probably for a pineapple sandwich. Maybe Dad was right. He was just a guy.

"Kids, come over here." Dad waved us toward him. "Terence Ackroyd just texted me the number of an investigator in Bolivia. I called and it's ringing."

Terence Ackroyd was the mystery writer who Sara had been due to meet in New York. After her luggage, cell phone, and passport all arrived from Bolivia without her, he was the one who'd told us Sara was missing.

Remembering what Galina Krause had said in Guam, we then put two and two together and realized that the Order had kidnapped Sara.

"One of Mr. Ackroyd's mystery novels is set in Bolivia, and he knows a first-rate private detective there," Dad said to us. "So he asked her to look into Sara's disappearance. He just sent me the number and told me to call her anytime—" He held up his hand. "Hello? Yes, this is Roald Kaplan," he said as softly as he could. "Terence Ackroyd gave me this number. Regarding . . . my wife. I was calling to see if you'd heard anything. . . ." His voice trailed off. I could tell he was listening intently. Then he put the phone on speaker, and we crowded around.

There was a woman's accented voice on the other end.

"Dr. Kaplan," she said huskily, "our team of nine investigators believes that Sara Kaplan was taken from Bolivia to Brazil. We are tracking her location now." Then her voice changed. "Mr. Ackroyd has insisted we do not contact official authorities. He has told you?"

"He has," my dad said, with a glance up at Darrell, who hung on every word. "He said there was a message in her luggage?"

"He can tell you more about that when you arrive in New York," the woman said. "In the meantime, we are on the brink of information that you will find helpful. I don't want to go too far, but it could be very good news. I will call you within the next several hours."

The expression on Dad's face was suddenly a mixture of tears and smiles. "That's really promising. I can't thank you enough for everything you're doing. Call this phone anytime. Please."

"Of course. Keep it close." She hung up.

Dad pressed the End Call button on his phone and put his arm around Darrell. He didn't say anything. Neither of them did. But for the first time since we'd learned about Sara's disappearance, Dad looked like he might really smile.

So did Darrell. "This is awesome! This is soooo good."

It was definitely not news to go all crazy happy about, not yet, but it felt good that real detectives were looking for Sara. "Our team of nine investigators," the woman had said. So far our little group had turned out to be pretty good at solving puzzles. But figuring out codes and riddles from the past was nothing like searching for a living person.

So, yeah, we felt lighter. I glanced around at the other passengers, wondering if they'd suddenly look less suspicious. They actually did.

Good. Now we could begin to relax a little.

The gate was cramming up even more now. There were so few empty seats that I didn't think anything when a man in a dark suit sat down in the row directly across from us. He was thin, and he wore thick black glasses and carried a green shoulder bag. His hands were stuck deep in his side pockets. I heard my dad's voice in my head—*Not everyone's planning something*—so I looked away.

Darrell was feeling better, which usually meant he was hungry. "I need a Snickers," he said. "Let's all go to the newsstand, me for food and you to search the world papers for tragedies. Okay, Dad?"

"Ten minutes," he said after checking his watch. "Stay close."

In one of his last messages to us, Uncle Henry had

predicted we'd hear about disasters happening around the world, and that they were connected to the Teutonic Order's hunt for the relics. Sure enough, we soon read reports of a building collapse in South America, a ship sinking in the Mediterranean, and the disappearance of a school bus that later reappeared, shot up by musket bullets from the nineteenth century.

Yeah. Try to figure that one out.

In the airport bookstore, we searched the papers as we always did, but my attention was instantly snagged by the shelf of Terence Ackroyd thrillers. Last week, I would've barely noticed them. The store had quite a few of them—*The Umbrian Vespers*, *The Berlin Manifesto*, and his latest hardcover novel, *The Mozart Inferno*, which was currently at the top of the bestseller list.

"He's an actual person," said Becca. "I almost doubted it until now. I should read one. We're going to see him in New York, after all." She decided on *The Prometheus Riddle*, a spy thriller set in Greece.

"A nuclear submarine sank off India's coast," Lily said, holding up that morning's London *Times*. "Ten crew members are missing. I bet the Order is behind it. They probably love to sink ships."

Darrell poked my arm. "If I move a fraction of an inch—"

"Your head will fall off?" I said.

"And . . . I can see the German dude, hovering outside my field of vision."

"Leathercoat," whispered Lily. "Call him Leather-coat."

Glancing over an issue of *Science* magazine, I saw the guy standing like a statue, holding a copy of *El Mundo* but not reading it.

I felt the same strange sensation I'd been experiencing for the last week: my skin tingled and a strange pain pierced my chest. It's the jab of adrenaline you feel when you're afraid. I'd felt that in my dream, too.

"I . . . have to use the bathroom," I said.

"Because you're scared," Darrell told me. "It's a well-known fact that panic makes you have to go—"

Lily put her hands over her ears. "Darrell, please stop talking!"

I headed to the men's room. "See you back at the gate."

"Nuh-uh. Buddy system," Becca said. "Darrell'll go with you."

"What are you, my kindergarten teacher?" Darrell said. "Last time I took a buddy to the bathroom, I was five years old. And while we're at it, why are we even calling it a *bath*room? It doesn't have a bathtub in it. That would be weird."

"You're weird," said Lily.

29

"Or a *rest*room," he went on, "because you don't go in there to rest."

"Darrell, please just go!" said Lily.

"That's it!" he said. "We should call it a go room! I love it."

She shoved him hard. "If you love it so much, then go to the go room already! Becca and I have our own mission." She held up her London *Times* and five dollars. "We're going to give the diary an old-fashioned makeover, a newspaper book cover!"

We split up, and Darrell tagged along with me. At least until his stomach remembered the Snickers he didn't get. "My taste buds are requesting multiple Snickerses for the road. Or the air. Or whatever. Wait for me here."

"Easy for you to say," I grumbled.

It was good to see him lightening up a bit. The phone call with the Bolivian detective had done it. We knew nothing about the investigation, but it occurred to me that if a team of detectives found Sara and got her on a plane, she might actually get to New York at the same time we did.

Meanwhile, I waited and waited until I couldn't wait anymore. I waved at Darrell at the candy counter; then I sprinted off down a long hall to the men's room. It smelled like disinfectant and hand soap once I got in there. I stood still for a few seconds, listening to gate announcements, until I was sure I was alone. I did what I needed to do, washed up, and was out again when a shape darkened the end of the corridor. "Darrell? It's about time—"

Not Darrell.

Leathercoat.

He stepped purposely down the narrow hall toward the restroom. I tried to move aside to give him room, but he blocked me.

"I'm sorry—" I started, but he raised his hand, then fixed a pair of lifeless eyes on mine.

CHAPTER FIVE

Leathercoat stood unmoving, staring right at me.

I could feel my scalp prickling. My forehead throbbed. My good feeling vanished completely. The man's irises were so dark, they seemed almost black. There was nothing in them but a kind of intense stillness.

"Wade Kaplan," he said softly, though his words managed to echo in the corridor, "you know whom I work for. You have met her. She injured your friend."

My hands instinctively balled into fists at the mention of Becca's wound and the thought of how much it was still hurting her. I remembered her from my dream, motionless on the floor of the cave.

"We knew you were with the Order," I said. "It was so obvious."

How many Snickerses is Darrell buying? Where is everyone?

"Then you know who Galina Krause has taken from you," Leathercoat said. "Kindly remember this fact the next time we meet, when I ask you for something."

His words were delivered slowly and with precision. He had just a trace of an accent, and his voice was deep and crisp, like an actor's.

"Because you have nothing better to do than follow us," I said.

"Allow me to pick your brain for a moment," he said. "Who do you imagine has the highest level of computing technology in the world?"

"What is this, a quiz?"

"Pretend it is."

I eyed the end of the corridor. I couldn't get to it. "NASA?" I answered.

He smiled thinly. "An appropriate response from an astronomer's son. NASA is to the Teutonic Order's Copernicus servers as a doghouse is to . . . Windsor Castle. Keep this in mind when you think to elude me and other agents of Galina Krause."

I couldn't think of anything to say besides "Whatever that means."

"You see, you and your family have no idea of the cosmic scope of what you have gotten yourselves involved in."

I stepped backward, bumping against the wall behind me. "You either," I said, meaninglessly.

"The great machine's relics? What has a simple family like yours to do with such treasures? Still, your cooperation may serve me well."

"Yeah, like we'd help you."

Darrell, come on and get in here! Really, in the whole airport, no one has to go to the go room?

"I could yell for help," I said.

"Sounding an alarm will do neither of us any good."

My fingers twitched. I wanted to hurt him somehow, to make him feel the terror that the Order made us feel. My hand dived into my backpack. Because it was shaking so much, it took me a second, but I finally whipped out one of the daggers. It felt wrong to be holding a deadly weapon, but I jabbed its short, wavy blade in the air anyway. It looked silly in my little hand. "Tell Galina to let Sara go."

He flicked his dead eyes at the dagger, then back to my face. "Perhaps you do not know French, but allow me to enlighten you," he said. "Galina Krause has given me *carte blanche*. This means 'blank check.' In other words, I may do as I wish. Wielding a dagger in this manner is impolite. Furthermore, it means nothing. You will not use it. You will never use it, Wade Kaplan."

"Stop saying my name!" I gripped the handle so

tightly my knuckles turned white. But he was right. I couldn't imagine using the dagger. How could I hurt a person? Even a bad one. I couldn't. I wouldn't.

"We will want both daggers also," he said. "But keep them for now, if it gives you comfort. We will meet again soon . . . Wade Kaplan."

All at once, the entrance to the corridor filled with shapes, and two young boys and their father trotted in, chattering and laughing. Before they saw me, the German strolled out past them, whistling a melody that sounded like a wolf howling.

I staggered out into the concourse. Fear rolled over me like the sweat dripping down my arms, my face. Darrell sauntered over from the snack stand, munching one Snickers bar while tearing open the wrapper of another. "I got one for you, but I had to eat it. . . . Dude, what's with you? Did the sink explode? You're dripping wet."

Barely able to stand on my own feet, I glared at him. "Thanks to you, I'm never using a bathroom again."

When we got back to the gate, Dad was flipping mad. "You never do things alone! I told you. Darrell—you messed up!"

"Dad, I'm sorry," he said. "The phone call was so good. . . ."

And more of the same, while I felt the blood drain from my face, neck, and head. I said, "I'm sorry, Dad. We're sorry. It was . . . I didn't expect he really was a Teutonic Knight. Dad, I'm scared. . . ."

He settled me quickly into his seat. "All right," he said more calmly, though his face was dark and anxious. "All right." He scanned the crowd, but of course Leathercoat was nowhere in sight. "Please tell me again exactly what he said. Word for word."

When I repeated Leathercoat's actual words, most of it sounded weirdly polite, almost friendly. I realized the menace was in what he *didn't* say. *Allow me to pick your brain . . . kindly remember this fact . . . allow me to enlighten you . . . if it gives you comfort.*

Dad listened intently, completely silent himself, as if, once more, he was trying to draw the whole incident into himself. Finally, he brushed my wet hair from my forehead. "Okay. Okay. You handled yourself very well."

"Should we tell security?" asked Becca. "Wade is scared, and so am I, Uncle Roald. Leathercoat says he wants us to cooperate? He's saying we can't tell anyone. Are we just going to do what he says?"

"No. No. I don't know." Dad looked around the busy gate and breathed sharply. "First, we'd have to prove something against him. Threatening is hard to prove, but it would certainly mean we wouldn't get to New

York for another few days. Look, I get it. Not contacting the police helps the Order as much as it might help us, but that's a risk we have to take, at least for now."

"Like Terence told us, and the investigator from Bolivia," said Lily.

"Exactly," he said. I saw his face grow more determined. He set his jaw and narrowed his eyes. "So, no police for now. But one way to look at this is that Leathercoat just blew his cover. He knows about us? Well, we know about him now, too."

I hoped that would help. Leathercoat had said we were in way over our heads. He was so right about that. I tried to swallow, tried to slow my pulse. I failed at both. Finally, with my hands quaking like leaves in the wind, I scribbled in my notebook. I wrote down everything I remembered of what Leathercoat said. Then I wrote down the sad dream. It was all pretty frightening stuff.

After what seemed like a century, the welcome announcement came.

"Now boarding Flight Five-Thirty-One to San Francisco and New York."

Good, I thought. *Get me out of this place.* I stuffed the notebook in my backpack and headed quickly into line.

CHAPTER SIX

The jet was packed. The attendant at the desk told my dad that the flight had been overbooked and that one of our five seats wasn't with the others. The loner was three rows back, which I said I would take, but Dad wanted us all together.

The man with the green shoulder bag was in the window seat across from our other seats. He already had a blanket draped over him and sat leaning against the window.

When another passenger—the long-haired acrobat guy who'd stood on his hand for the baby—came in, heading for the open aisle seat, Dad asked if he'd mind switching with me.

"Or are you two together?" Dad asked him.

"No, no." The acrobat glanced at the man by the window, then at me, and smiled. "Not at all. Please, son, sit here."

So after we were settled, Darrell and I were split by the aisle. He only took his seat—he was the last one to sit before the cabin door closed—after making sure Leathercoat wasn't on our flight. "I didn't see him. But if he works for Galina, he's too good to be seen." Which didn't make any real sense, and didn't slow my pounding heart, either.

As the jet taxied from the gate to the runway, the man with the green bag turned to me. "I am Dominic Chen," he said, extending his right hand.

His fingers were ice-cold. "Wade Kaplan," I said.

"I like to sleep on overnight flights," he said with a slender smile, "but the protocol with fellow passengers is to chat, so we can, if you like."

Protocol.

A week ago, *protocol* was just a school vocabulary word. But since Uncle Henry's death had set off the secret Frombork Protocol—a set of instructions for the Guardians to gather the relics and destroy them—the word had taken on a whole new meaning. Maybe Mr. Chen's use of *protocol* was just a coincidence.

Coincidence. Another word that sounded an alarm.

"That's okay," I said. "I like to rest, too."

He nodded. "When we awake, it will be Sunday morning, the first day of a brand-new week. Enjoy your sleep."

There was something soothing about Mr. Chen's voice. Within minutes of hearing it, and the droning engines, I began to feel drowsy. I glanced at Darrell, the girls, and my dad. Their eyes were closed. We'd all gone a long time without any kind of rest, so that was good.

I closed my eyes, too. I wanted to go back to the dream of the cave, if only to get a better ending to it, but returning to a dream is nearly impossible when you try to force it. It didn't work. Soon enough I stopped hearing noises and fell sound asleep.

I dreamed of nothing this time. Black space. No sound.

A few hours later, I woke up to bad news.

". . . affects passengers with destinations in New York," the pilot was saying. "A real kahuna of a snowstorm is flying up the East Coast and has shut down all three New York airports."

Lots of passengers groaned, so we weren't alone.

"Are you kidding me?" Darrell's hair was going in every direction. He was obviously still groggy, but he had the ability to be groggy and jumpy at the same time. "We're finally on our way, then everything stops?

I can't take this!" He slammed both fists onto his thighs.

"Don't self-punch," I said.

"But come on—"

"I get it," I said. "Two steps forward, one step back." I glanced at Dad, who leaned over and said something quietly. Darrell wiped his eyes and mumbled a couple of words, but shook his head sharply.

Soon there was a flurry of additional announcements.

"We'll arrive a half hour ahead of schedule . . . it's raining in San Francisco . . . airport hotel for stranded passengers . . ."

Blah blah blah. Landing early was normally good, except this time it meant that we'd spend an extra half hour in rainy San Francisco before we could get to New York and start our real search for Sara.

My ears popped as the jet descended. Mr. Chen was still wrapped up in his blanket, eyes closed, face turned to the window. Even with the clouds, the shade next to him was brightening with daylight. I wanted to raise it to see the city as we landed, like we were getting somewhere, but I didn't want to bother him.

The landing gear rumbled welcomingly beneath the floor. As we drew closer to the airport, the pilot said his final words to the flight crew to prepare for landing. I tapped Mr. Chen's shoulder lightly.

"Excuse me, Mr. Chen, we're landing. If you're going to New York, there's a snowstorm." I waited for him to rustle his blanket, blink, turn to face me sleepily. But he didn't move.

We were asked to shift our seat backs upright. Because Mr. Chen remained sleeping, a passing flight attendant pressed the button on the arm of his seat to push his seat back gently forward. As she moved down the aisle, the blanket over his shoulders rolled down a few inches, and my blood turned to ice.

In the folds of Mr. Chen's neck were several dark bruises.

"Mr. Chen?" I whispered. "Mr. Chen?" My throat seized. I could barely make a sound. I leaned across the aisle. "Dad," I croaked. "Dad!" I glanced back to make sure I had seen what I thought I had.

There was no doubt. The angle of his neck and the purple marks on his skin meant only one thing.

I was sitting next to a dead man.

CHAPTER SEVEN

Dominic Chen was dead.

What I mean is, he was dead *now*, but he wasn't before. He'd been very much alive when I'd gone to sleep a few hours earlier.

I had never been so close to death before. He was so still. His eyes, his lips—his whole body was sunken heavily into his seat as if he were made of stone. The dream image of Becca on the floor of the cave flashed in my mind, then vanished.

My dad couldn't leave his seat while the jet taxied to the gate, and it took its time getting there. "Wade," he whispered across Darrell. "Keep still. Don't freak out. I'll be there as soon as . . ."

I wanted to tell him *easy for you to say*, but my mouth

wasn't working. It was the longest eight minutes of my life. Becca, Lily, and Darrell shot me astonished looks, as if they understood only too well that my seatmate was dead. Had we changed this much already? That we expected somebody to die so close to us? I didn't want to believe it.

I tried my hardest not to throw up. I wanted to run screaming down the aisle, but I was cemented where I sat.

Finally, the seat belt sign binged off. Becca bolted up in her seat, one hand over her open mouth, while Lily held her other one. Dad carefully but quickly eased his way between the passengers already crowding the aisle and helped me out of my belt.

I could barely stand up, but we managed to exchange seats. Dad bent over Mr. Chen in a position that blocked most passengers' view. I heard him whisper a few words and nod as if he'd gotten a response. Totally crazy, I thought, but I knew I wasn't exactly thinking straight. He was being careful. He didn't want people to panic. Or us to panic. When Dad turned his face up, his eyes were filled with fear, but his lips wore a thin smile meant to keep anyone else from suspecting that Mr. Chen was dead. Why?

No police. No authorities. Not even now.

Becca's eyes were welling up. "Is he . . ."

"Don't say the word, please," Dad said, tucking the blanket gently behind Mr. Chen's shoulders, as if he were simply asleep.

"He said *protocol*," I whispered to no one in particular. "Nobody uses that word. Not to a kid. But he said it." I must have had a sick look on my face, because in the middle of everyone moving, opening the overhead bins, talking, Becca put her good arm around me.

Lily poked Darrell. "You told us Leathercoat wasn't here."

Darrell looked as terrified as I felt, jerking his head in every direction. "I didn't see him. I checked and rechecked."

We were being careful, not raising our voices, not leaving our seats. My heart was thundering; my ears rang. Passengers streamed down the aisles. I guess we appeared as though we were waiting for them to leave. When most of them had, we gathered our stuff and looked one last time at Mr. Chen, and my dad steered us off the plane into the Jetway.

"We have to tell someone," Becca said softly, wiping her cheeks. "Maybe airport security?" I was carrying her bag again, and I touched her hand for a second as we came out into the gate.

"In a minute." Dad scanned the passengers as they made their way down the concourse. "Telling the authorities might be uncomfortable for the Order, if the police even believe they did this—"

"They did!" said Lily.

"—but we were sitting next to him," he continued. "And the investigation will keep us here. I know it sounds callous—cruel, even—but we can't get drawn into this any more than we have to be. We didn't actually know Mr. Chen. It could be unrelated."

"Dad, no," I said, as calmly as I could. "First there's Leathercoat; then Mr. Chen said *protocol*. Maybe he wanted to see if I would do or say anything. But I didn't. Maybe I should've . . . I don't know . . ."

"Everyone, just stop. For a second," Dad said. "I'm sorry; I mean . . . we're obviously not playing around here. You know that."

I thought we knew it, but I guess there was more to learn. Dad had never wanted us to get mixed up in whatever this was becoming. From the murder of Uncle Henry to Sara's kidnapping, it was way more dangerous than anything we'd thought possible. Now here we were, at an airport in a strange city, and a man sitting next to us had been murdered.

The chubby, laughing baby's parents settled him into his stroller, as he bubbled with giggles. The last few passengers exited the Jetway, some on their phones, others chatting with one another.

"They're all too busy to notice Mr. Chen," Darrell said. "They don't care about him just sitting there being all—"

"Don't say it." I could hardly suck in enough air to breathe, and my head was light.

"—murdered," Darrell continued. "Maybe he saw Leathercoat follow you to the go room and made the connection."

Dad's phone buzzed. He opened it. "The airline about the delay."

Then the man who'd joked with the baby and whose seat I had taken hurried out of the Jetway. His face was tight as he scanned every direction around him. When he saw us looking, he tried to put on a calmer face, even smiling, though it was easy to see the strain.

"Did everyone see that?" Lily said softly. "He's trying not to look worried. He must have noticed that Mr. Chen was dead."

"The flight crew discovered him," Becca said shakily. "Look."

The woman who had pushed his seat upright rushed out of the Jetway to the attendants at the gate. The microphone thumped when she covered it with her hand. Her face was pale. She whispered a few words to them, and one made a call on his walkie-talkie. We just stood against the wall pretending not to watch. Soon a small group of security officers and airline officials converged at the gate. A pair of EMTs rolled in a gurney, and one of the attendants announced that there would be a delay before the next flight could depart.

Then we saw him.

Leathercoat.

He strolled toward our gate from the opposite end of the concourse, a few paces behind the EMT folks. My spine went cold.

"Was he on our flight or not?" asked Lily.

"Not," said Darrell. "Unless he can make himself invisible."

Leathercoat stopped amid the commotion. He listened to the security officers and raised his phone. He spoke into it, then hung up.

Becca frowned. "Hold on. If it was his mission to kill Mr. Chen, why would he hang around? He'd already be out on the street."

The German man turned, glanced casually at me, and walked down the concourse from where he'd come, passing two uniformed policemen and a third in a rumpled blazer, who headed straight for the gate.

"What you're saying is that there was another killer on the plane," said Lily. "What are we, surrounded by killers?"

"Of course we are," Darrell grumbled.

Dad ended his phone call with the airline just as airport security made an announcement over the intercom, requesting that all the passengers from our flight remain in the terminal for questioning.

"Wait here, okay?" he said, retrieving our passports from his bag. "I'll talk to the officers right now. Tell them about the seat swap. You stay here. I want to get off their list of suspects ASAP."

We watched for a few tense minutes as Dad spoke to the detective in charge. We tried to read the officer's face, but it was a blank. He nodded and took a lot of notes. Behind them, several officers were huddled in the corridor near a snack kiosk, talking among themselves.

Lily nudged Darrell. "Don't you need another Snickers?"

He shrugged. "No, I'm good. Two is my limit."

Lily rolled her eyes. "I mean, go listen to the police."

"Me? Why don't you go?" Darrell asked.

"Because I don't eat chocolate."

Darrell narrowed his eyes at her. "Who doesn't eat chocolate? And what does chocolate have to do with it if you just want to spy—"

"Can you eat another candy bar or not?" Lily said.

"Yes, yes, of course!" he growled.

Darrell casually walked past the officers. Filling his

hands with candy, he leaned over to listen. Dad came back from the officers.

"Wade, I told them *some* of what Mr. Chen said to you," he said, keeping an eye on Darrell at the snack kiosk. "Small talk only. It wasn't everything, but it was enough for them to believe we had nothing to do with . . . what happened."

He removed his glasses and polished them quickly on his sleeve. With the glasses off, it was easier to see the worry in his eyes. "Because of the snowstorm, the flight's rescheduled for ten tomorrow morning. They've booked two rooms for us. But it seems too easy for the German to find us. I have another hotel in mind."

After a minute or two in line, Darrell strolled over, unwrapping what I counted as his third Snickers of the day. "I discovered three things," he said. "One, Mr. Chen was from Hong Kong."

"We guessed that," said Becca.

"Two, his neck was broken from behind."

"From behind?" My stomach poured up into my throat. "The killer reached over the seat and killed him? While I was sleeping there?"

Darrell nodded. "It's not safe to sleep on a plane."

"What was the third thing?" asked Lily.

He bit off a chunk of candy bar. "Mr. Chen's hand was missing."

There was a minute of stunned silence as we watched Darrell chew.

Dad narrowed his eyes. "Darrell . . . what?"

"Mr. Chen had a fake hand," he said. "What do you call those?"

"A prosthetic. He had a prosthetic hand?" Dad replied. "I didn't notice it."

"Well, he had one, and now it's gone. The police figure someone stole it, because it's not, you know, attached to him anymore."

Mr. Chen had had his left hand in his pocket the first time I saw him, and I remembered how he'd already covered himself with a blanket when I took my seat next to him. No wonder we hadn't noticed.

"But why on earth . . . I don't understand this," Dad said, hoisting his carry-on over his shoulder and moving away from the gate. "Anyway, we can leave now. The police have my number if they need to ask any more questions."

We followed him quietly along the concourse and down the escalator to the baggage claim area on the ground floor, when he paused as if he'd just thought of something.

"Is Leathercoat here again?" Lily asked, swiveling her head around.

"No," Dad said. "And that's the point. Before we go,

there's something I want to do. Kids, I think we should leave Vela and the daggers here at the airport."

For a minute, I thought I'd heard him wrong. "Dad, what? Leave Vela. And the daggers? No way. They're all far too valuable—"

"Which is exactly my point," he said, lowering his voice to a whisper. "Now that we know that the German is here in San Francisco, whether he followed us here or not, I think Vela—and all of us—will be safer if we store it in a secure public place. A place that we're going to come back to, but one that's well protected." He nodded behind us.

A sign on the wall next to an office door read: Airport Travel Agency Baggage Storage.

"I've used this kind of service before," Dad explained. "We can leave a bag here with Vela and the daggers locked up inside. It's one of the safest and most anonymous methods of storing something."

"Don't they search everything?" I asked.

"They'll x-ray our bag to make sure there's nothing dangerous inside, but not hand-search it. The special holster will hide the daggers, and Vela will look like any sort of jewelry. Only we can retrieve them. Look, it's an international airport, so their security has to be tight."

"You're right, Uncle Roald," said Lily, looking up from her cell phone. "There's a website that rates these things, and it says this is one of the best. Besides, if Leathercoat already left the airport, he won't know we hid the stuff here."

"I agree," Becca said with a quick nod, "but I'm keeping the diary. It's disguised as a schoolbook anyway."

It felt so wrong to leave Vela behind after we'd searched half the world to find it, but I remembered what Leathercoat had said to me, and Dad's plan made sense. Besides, I didn't want to believe that the San Francisco airport was in the pocket of the Teutonic Order of Ancient Prussia.

"Yeah, okay," I said.

Lily had a small bag that could be zipped closed and locked with a tiny padlock. We holstered up both daggers in there, and we left Vela in its velvet wrapper, twisted inside one of Dad's sweaters. We handed it over the counter to a pleasant older woman. At the last minute, Darrell decided to stuff his spare Snickers bars in. He whispered to us that they would distract any thieves. Thieves like him, I thought.

It took a few minutes, and it was done. I clutched the baggage-claim ticket in my hand and then shoved it deep into my jacket pocket.

Walking away from the storage office felt strange and still a little wrong. I turned to look back. A young couple was stowing a folding baby stroller with the same woman who had helped us. She said something to them and they laughed. I felt better.

Then through the windows I saw the gurney being rolled along the sidewalk to an ambulance. It had a black body bag strapped on it. I felt worse again.

Outside the terminal, it was morning, and the air was different—colder, grayer. It was raining, as the pilot had predicted. A wet Sunday morning. Mr. Chen had said it would be Sunday when we woke. The beginning of a new week. Not for him, it wouldn't. I felt heavy inside. I barely knew him, but a man I had talked to was now dead.

Why?

Had Vela brought a Guardian and a Teutonic Knight to San Francisco, or was there another relic here? Would we find out, or get to New York before anything happened? Would anyone else die?

I only knew one thing. We couldn't let Galina Krause win.

As we headed for the taxi stand, I found that the rain was steadier and harder than I'd thought, and that every single cab was taken.

Every cab but one.

CHAPTER EIGHT

A beat-up old car idled at the end of the covered taxi area, its driver leaning back as if he were the only thing holding it up. He was a short, round man with a grizzly-bear beard. The car was big and black, from years ago, and dinged up from bumper to bumper.

"That's an old hackney cab," my father said. "Like they have in London. It's strange to see a vintage one here."

"The driver looks pretty vintage, too," Lily commented, "which means he probably knows his way around and will get us to our hotel so we can sleep and eat but mostly sleep, which I need to do."

"Let's snag him before anyone else," said Darrell. He led us at a brisk trot to the end of the taxi stand, where

Dad told the driver our destination.

The guy squinted at us up and down and tugged on his scraggly beard. "I don't drive kids around."

"Excuse me?" said Dad. "You can't mean that."

The man scowled. "Sure I do."

"Oh, now please. You're the last one, it's raining, we're tired—"

"So sleep," the man mumbled. "Go on. Beat it."

We were all stunned. No one had ever talked to us that way. Finally, Dad turned back to the terminal. "We'll find the shuttle."

"Rude!" said Lily.

"Yeah, thanks a lot," Darrell grunted as he spun around with us. Then he froze. He stared into the passenger window of the cab at—of all things—an electric guitar belted in the seat like a living person.

"A vintage Strat!" Darrell gasped. He plays guitar, and knows all the famous ones. "Can I take a look?"

The cabbie said, "No!" but Darrell's hands had a mind of their own. They reached in through the open window, formed a chord on the fret board, and strummed it. It sounded awful.

"Hey, this is strung all wrong—"

"*You're* all wrong!" the driver said, swatting Darrell's hands away. "Get your fingers off that. It's strung for a lefty."

"Darrell, come on," Dad said, his hand on Darrell's shoulder.

"Oh, like Hendrix," Darrell said, spinning away from Dad.

"You wish. Now get! Get!" The scruffy man flicked his fingers at us dismissively and then plopped down into the driver's seat—which because it was an English car was on the wrong side, too—then threw the cab into gear and put-putted off in a cloud of blue smoke.

"What a . . ." Becca didn't say the word, but I guessed it. "That was the last cab!"

"Was that the weirdest thing ever?" Lily hissed through her teeth. "Why does that guy even *drive* the junky old taxi if he's not going to use it as a taxi?"

"Never mind, never mind." My dad let out a deep sigh that ended in a sort of laugh. "If he doesn't want to drive us, he doesn't want to drive us. I'm sure there's a shuttle that will bring us downtown."

We backtracked to the shuttle platform, where Darrell stomped back and forth, shaking his head, until the bus finally swung around the corner toward us. The shuttle was already crammed with passengers, so Darrell and I stood until seats opened up at the next stop.

It would take, the driver said, "only about forty-five or fifty minutes to reach your hotel in the city."

"Only," Becca grumbled, setting her bag on the floor

tightly between her feet. "Let's just call it an hour."

It turned out to be longer than that. After an endless series of looping roads that took us past all the airport's terminals at least once, we coasted onto a multilane highway heading north. Picking up some speed, but not much, the shuttle skirted a range of dirt-brown hills with scrubby tufts growing here and there. Then we split off in the slowest way possible to a highway that crossed the lower end of what Dad said was San Francisco Bay.

"I've never been to San Francisco before," Lily said, gazing through windows that were still streaming with rain. "Anyone?"

Dad nodded slowly, turning from the windows to us. "Darrell, your mom knows this city well. She wanted me to visit, so we spent our first anniversary here." He smiled a sad smile. "Sara really loves San Fran."

Darrell wiped his nose. We all felt some Sara grief coming, but this wasn't the place or time, so we stared out the window for a while.

"That's the Golden Gate Bridge, isn't it?" Becca pointed to our left, where we could just see the huge structure looming out of the mist.

"Sure is," the driver called back to us. "Weather here changes by the half hour. It'll clear up this afternoon. You'll get a good view."

The rest of us only knew the basic stuff that everybody knows about San Francisco. The Gold Rush put it on the map in 1849. Cable cars ran up and down the crazy-hilly streets. Its Chinatown was enormous; there were some nifty skyscrapers, cool painted houses, and, of course, Alcatraz, the old prison on an island in the bay.

Outside of Dad, none of us had ever been there before, so technically it was a strange city. Still, after a week hopping around Europe and the Pacific, it was a relief to be back home in the US.

Even if we were stranded here.

And the Teutonic Order knew it.

The driver seemed to be weaving a giant loop, letting people off every few blocks. Finally, he circled back to Sutter Street, where he stopped in front of a narrow, five-floor, yellow-brick building, and we piled out onto the sidewalk. The Hotel Topaz had window balconies on the facade and a fire escape zigzagging down the front to the street.

"I chose the Topaz because it's under the radar," Dad told us as we entered. "And it was where Sara and I stayed." Which seemed as good a reason as any. Sara was a huge part of everything we did now.

The ponytailed guy at the registration desk said we were early for check-in time, but luckily our rooms were available. He gave us keys. The girls were in the room right next to Dad, Darrell, and me, with a door connecting us. We'd had that arrangement in Berlin, too.

Becca and Lily checked out their room to wash up and to look at Becca's cut. When they came back, Dad called us together for a talk.

"Kids, listen. The Order is here for us or for something else. Either way, none of you goes anywhere without the others, and not unless I know about it. No repeats of Honolulu." He glared at me and Darrell.

We all nodded.

"In the meantime, I'll pick us up something to eat," he added. "I'm starving and I'm sure you are, too. Don't leave the room, and don't let anyone in. I'll call only if I have to tell you something."

"What about Mom?" Darrell asked. "Can we call the investigator or Terence Ackroyd? Get an update on what's going on?"

"Definitely," said Dad, opening his phone. "I was going to call Terence when I got back anyway, but you can. I'm forwarding his number to you. It'll be good for you to talk to him. Tell him our flight's delayed until morning and that I'll call him right back."

He gave Darrell a tired smile that I figured was meant to be encouraging. I needed that, too. I couldn't stop seeing Mr. Chen lifeless in his seat. One person was dead already. One person so far.

"Okay, Dad," I said. "Hurry back."

He smiled at each of us separately, opened the door, slid out, and closed it gently behind him.

Everyone was quiet for a few minutes before Darrell nervously dialed Terence Ackroyd. We watched his face wrinkle as the call went to voice mail, but he actually seemed relieved. He flipped the phone shut. "He's probably out investigating," he said.

"You know it," said Becca.

I slipped my hand into the right pocket of my jacket to check on Vela's baggage-claim ticket. I felt a moment of panic when my finger poked into a little hole in the lining.

"Oh, no—"

"What?" said Lily.

A moment later, I felt the ticket . . . and something else.

I slid off the jacket. "There's something in here. . . ."

"He bugged you!" said Darrell. "I knew it. Leather-coat put something in your pocket when you were in the go room, and now he knows where we are!"

I spread the jacket on the bed. "He never got near me. Not that you or your Snickers would know." The object, whatever it was, was caught in the folds of the lining, and I worked it up through the hole and out into my fingers. "Whoa, what's this . . . ?"

It was a flat, round piece of something hard and shiny like ceramic, and it had a vein of pale green stone coiling through the design.

"Omigod, that's white jade," said Lily, snatching it from me. "I have earrings made from jade like that. This is beautiful. Where did you . . . Wade, are you a secret shoplifter?"

"What? No!"

"Then where did you—" She gasped. "Is this a gift for Becca?"

"What?"

"Lily!" Becca screamed.

"Give it to me!" said Darrell. He swiped it from Lily's palm and held it out for all of us to study. The piece was highly polished and perfectly circular, about two inches across. The jade design on the top appeared to be the body of an animal, but it wasn't all there. The flip side was crisscrossed with metallic fibers, and the edge of the bottom side was ridged with tiny teeth, like the edge of a quarter, only much deeper.

All this time, Lily was tapping on her phone. "Hang on, I'm looking it up . . . looking . . . and . . . here. It's Chinese, and it's called a tile." She turned the screen around so we could look at some photos. "These are a bunch of others."

"Those are not new," said Becca. "They're works of art, from museums. Is yours valuable, Wade?"

"I don't know," I said. "And it's not *mine*. I don't know how it got in my jacket."

"So then where did it . . ." Darrell stopped and stared at us. "Whoa!" he said. "Whoa! Mr. Chen! He slipped it into your pocket before he died, then he died, and now you have it. That's it. I solved it!"

"Darrell, wait." I thought back to the shuttle ride, the airports, the flights, the crowds. No one had touched me, brushed up against me, done anything near me, except my family. The only time I was even close enough for a stranger to get into my jacket pocket was on the flight from Honolulu.

"Actually, you're right," I said. "Mr. Chen must have slipped this tile to me when I was sleeping."

CHAPTER NINE

Dominic Chen.

Now his death was frightening in a whole other way. As nice as he had seemed, as friendly as his smile had been, I felt so creeped out imagining his fingers in my jacket pocket while I slept. The fingers that would soon be dead.

"Wade, are you all right?" Lily was searching my face.

"He's fine," said Darrell. "He always looks a little sick."

"If he did slip this to me, how did he know for sure I was, you know, one of them?" I said. "We're not wearing signs, are we? It doesn't say 'Guardian' on my forehead, does it?"

Darrell leaned close to examine my head. "I make out *G-E-E-K*—"

"Ha. Ha," I said.

"Maybe Guardians know about us through their network, or from Carlo in Bologna," Becca said. "Or maybe Mr. Chen didn't know for sure about us, but he was in danger, so he hid the tile on you."

"Right," said Lily. "If he hadn't been . . . if he hadn't died, maybe he would've found us and told us all about it once we landed."

I turned the piece over in my fingers. It was cool to the touch, and it certainly felt old, like Lily's web search suggested. But it gave off none of the same feeling that Vela did.

Touching a true relic of Copernicus's astrolabe was like nothing I'd ever experienced before. When I'd held Vela in the cave, the tingle across the surface of my skin and into my chest was like I'd been plugged into an outlet. I could barely take in air. Vela in my palm had felt heavier than heavy, and it made perfect sense—I was holding part of an ancient time machine! Here, no. It was a tile, maybe old, almost definitely a clue, but not one of the relics.

But there was a chance it was also a key that would lead us to one. Like the Copernicus dagger had led us to Vela.

As I studied the tile by the window, I saw that our bus driver had been right. The rain had stopped, and the mist was beginning to burn off, now that it was getting close to noon. I turned to the others.

"Here's what I think," I said. "I think Leathercoat is after this tile, whatever it means, and if he wasn't on our flight, then another agent of the Order killed Mr. Chen for it. We have to think that *both* that killer and Leathercoat are after us for *both* Vela and this tile."

"Which kind of explains why Leathercoat just warned you in Honolulu," Becca added. "And didn't try anything worse—"

The room phone buzzed loudly on the desk by the window.

We stared at it like it was a tarantula.

"Who's calling the room?" Darrell whispered as if the person on the other end could hear. "Dad would call our phones."

There was a long silence as we waited for a second ring. It didn't come. Becca let out a long breath. "Maybe it just was a wrong—"

Zzzt! Zzzt! The phone somehow sounded more urgent than before.

"It could be the front desk, asking if we have enough shampoo," Lily said. "If we don't answer, they'll send someone up. . . ."

It buzzed again. No one went for it.

"Really?" Lily rolled her eyes and picked it up. "Hello?"

You could hear someone's voice on the other end. It was soft, low. Lily's eyes widened. She pulled the phone away from her face, searched the keypad, and pressed a button. "He wants it on speaker."

"Who does?" asked Darrell.

"Can the four of you hear me?" asked a deep voice.

"It's him!" I said, putting my palm over the microphone. "The German! Leathercoat!" I removed my hand. "What do you want?"

"You will please go to the window."

"Omigod, now what?" Lily whispered.

We lifted the narrow blinds. On the opposite sidewalk, in front of a doorway with an awning over it, stood the tall man with white hair. He was gazing up at our window as he spoke into his cell phone.

"First, I must compliment you on your ability to appear at the right place and at the right time. Copernicus himself would have approved. Now look down the street to my left."

We did. The sidewalks were crowded, though the cars were few. Darrell pointed. "Dad's down there. I see him coming."

Two blocks away, my father was carrying two paper

shopping bags—the food he had promised to bring back to the room.

"You see now what easy prey you and your family are."

My dad was ambling up the street toward a killer he didn't know was there. It was sickening. I wanted to pound on the window to warn him. "Someone call him—"

"Call him if you like, but I will be gone."

"So you're just going to keep haunting us? Like some creepy ghost?" said Lily as she tapped on her phone. "It's ringing."

We saw Dad pause, shift his food bags, and fumble for his phone.

"Soon I will ask you for Vela," Leathercoat said casually, "as well as the item you received from Mr. Chen. I will pursue you without end to obtain what I want. Cooperate, or your father will be connected to Mr. Chen's demise. Vela will be seized from you. You will have nothing. Darrell will tell you that one person dear to you has already been taken. You do not wish to make it a pair."

"Why you—" Darrell screamed.

"Uncle Roald!" Lily yelled into the phone. "Leathercoat is outside the hotel!"

Dad started running up the street.

Click.

The call ended.

Leathercoat stepped back under the awning, and I swear the shadows enveloped him. I wasn't sure whether he actually slipped through the building's open door or just dematerialized. I'd have believed either. Dad ran past the spot and charged over to the hotel. Seconds later, he rushed into the room, and we leaped on him.

"Leathercoat was right down there!" I cried. "He saw you and threatened to do something to you if we didn't hand over Vela and the jade tile. He said he would find us."

Dad double-locked the door. "But are you all right?"

"We're fine," Lily said. "Just . . . scared."

"I think we should call the police," Becca said. "He said we shouldn't, but he's threatening you, and all of us. We have to."

Dad shook his head sharply. "Hold on. Back up. You said something about a jade tile? What tile?"

I handed it to him. "Mr. Chen passed it to me before he died. Leathercoat said so."

Dad studied the tile in silence, and then went to the window. "This Leathercoat man is using us—using *you.* Twice now he's talked to you kids instead of me. I'm sorry he's doing this to you, but he's relying on our fear about Sara to keep his actions secret." He looked in our eyes one after the other. "It's smart of him. He's right that broadcasting what he's doing would hinder us, too. So, fine. We'll be quiet. For now.

"But we won't play into his hands, either."

Dad's words made me remember a theme we had studied in Language Arts, the struggle between good and evil. Leathercoat was like an evil demon, a devil, luring us into doing his work for him. It made me feel guilty and a little sick to my stomach.

"Can we at least change hotels?" Lily asked. "Leathercoat is a ghoul. He scares me way more than Darrell when he talks about the go room. Plus, who knows if he has reinforcements coming? Leathercoat, I mean. He'll attack us in our sleep."

"No, he won't," said Darrell. "I'll kill him first!"

"Darrell, never say that," Dad said. "That's what the Order wants."

"Well, we're *doing* what they want," Darrell said, a bit more calmly. "We should just go back to the airport and wait. Not play his stupid game. We have to find Mom—"

"Except, wait . . . ," I started. Darrell shot me a glare, but I went on. "Look, we can't get to New York until tomorrow at the earliest. If there's a relic here, yeah, we could let the Order just find it. Leathercoat would bring it to Galina. Or we could try for it ourselves."

Dad rubbed his forehead, then turned to me. "But, Wade . . ."

"No, Dad, listen. If Leathercoat wants this tile, then it's a clue to a new relic. Mr. Chen thought we could find the relic, or he wouldn't have given this to me. I think he knew we were Guardians. And anyway, wouldn't *two* relics be better than one to help us get Sara back?"

Darrell held his breath during my rant. He breathed it out slowly, then looked up at Dad. "I think Wade's right. And you know how hard that is for me to say."

Dad stood there, staring out the window, then at each of our faces. I was actually surprised, but Lily and Becca were both nodding, as if agreeing with what Darrell and I had said.

"All right," said Dad. "We *are* stuck here until morning. So, yes. We can follow this clue—if it *is* a clue—except that we stop at the slightest hint of more danger. Either way, relic or no relic, we are on our flight at ten tomorrow morning. Agreed?"

"Agreed," said Lily.

"Besides, we already have Vela and Copernicus's magical diary and two priceless daggers," said Becca. "After everything that's happened, we *must* be doing something right. And no matter how scary it gets, we sort of have to keep on doing it. For Sara. And for Copernicus."

Which was not something Becca would have said before last week. She was becoming a little tougher, different. I noticed it in myself, too. The old Wade would never have had the nerve to pull a dagger on a man. The truth was that the search for the relics was changing us. Who we'd end up being, I couldn't tell yet. But one thing was certain.

We had just agreed to work outside the law.

Dad scanned the street one last time and then lowered the blinds. "The first thing we do is to leave the hotel. The second thing is to get this tile examined by an expert—"

"The Asian Art Museum," said Lily, waving her cell phone at us. "They're open till seven tonight. We can walk there in half an hour."

We wolfed down the food Dad had brought. The few minutes of eating helped to make us feel a little more normal, even if we weren't.

I stood up. "Let's go. The more we know, the more we know."

"That's deep, bro," Darrell said. "Can I quote you?"

"I'd let you, but I own all the rights to what I say."

We grabbed our gear and vacated the hotel, leaving our keys but nothing else in the rooms. We didn't inform the ponytailed clerk that we were checking out. I guess you could say that this was our new way, being sneaky about what we did.

We were playing the Order's game now.

Using a map Becca snatched from the front desk as we left, we headed down the next two blocks then turned onto Larkin Street. It was dry for the moment and warmer. I kept swiveling around, but naturally didn't spot Leathercoat.

"He doesn't need to follow us," Darrell said, guessing what I was thinking as only a stepbrother can. "He'll wait for us to come to him."

"He knew right where we were," said Becca. "Can you really trace a phone right to a single room in a city?"

"It's possible," said my dad, "but not with another cell phone. He must be getting computing help somewhere."

"Leathercoat mentioned all the computers that the Order has," I said. "They probably have their own satellites in orbit."

"I'd like to put him in orbit," said Lily.

Becca nodded. "After I do."

Twenty minutes later, we reached the Asian Art Museum. It was a large, imposing structure, a kind of Greek temple on one side of a large grassy square. Banners featuring its current exhibits flapped above the entrance as if to beckon us in.

Wondering what we might learn about the tile that,

small as it was, had already claimed a life, we made our way up the wide steps to the front doors.

We took one last look around, then entered the museum.

CHAPTER TEN

Even before we paid, Becca made a beeline for the information counter. It was a glass-topped desk staffed by two men in muted jackets with name tags pinned to them. She leafed through brochures and maps of the different collections. She'd already told me she collected brochures from places she visited.

"You get a lot of information from them," she'd said.

Dad paid student prices for us, full for him, all in cash.

I glanced out the door. Darrell did, too. The early-afternoon sun was emerging from behind the clouds and flashing off the puddles dotting the square.

"Changeable weather, all right," he said. "It almost looks nice."

"So do you," I said. "Almost." He shoved me.

Becca glanced up from her museum map and pointed to the main staircase. "Third floor is where the Chinese galleries are."

We headed up.

"If I remember, the dynasty of Ming emperors ruled from around the thirteenth century through the six-teenth, certainly during the time Copernicus lived," Dad said.

"Fourteenth to the sixteenth." Becca squinted closely at the brochure's tiny type. "From 1368 to 1644. The Ming court was said to be one of the most advanced in its arts and weapons."

"Did Copernicus ever make it to China?" Darrell said, hiking up two steps at a time. "Dad, do you know?"

"I don't think it's in his biography," he said, "but then neither are a lot of things we're finding out. There were trade routes, though."

"I could look it up in three seconds," said Lily. "But I don't want to. Wasn't there something called the Slick Road?"

"No," I said.

"The *Silk* Road was what they called the trade route from China to Europe," said Becca. She flipped the bro-chure over. "People in Italy, Portugal, and Spain traded silk and spices and goods with China from Marco Polo's time on. It was a big business when Copernicus lived."

"Is all that in the brochure?" I asked.

"Part of that was my very own, and I own all the rights." She smiled, then lowered her voice. "I bet if I can figure out the key words, the diary will tell us exactly where Copernicus traveled."

And where we'd have to follow him and his Guardians.

With each step we'd taken so far—to Berlin, Bologna, Rome, Guam, and every place in between—we'd discovered more and more about the great astronomer. The shadows of his life were clearing, mist by mist. It was no wonder he'd seemed so real in *the dream*.

Lily spotted the Ming galleries first, and zipped ahead of us.

The polished floorboards reflected the soothing overhead lights, and the quiet, nearly deserted rooms— featuring statues, pottery, scrolls, and carvings of wood, bone, and ivory—were strangely calming.

Becca felt it. I could tell by the way she relaxed her wounded arm. She knew, as we all did, that the Order was out there waiting for us. How could we not? But for the moment, being in the museum comforted us. It was full of the aura of caring for the past as if it were—as we knew it actually *was*—a living thing. It seemed pretty obvious, as we walked into the galleries, that the relic quest was drawing us in again.

"Let's ask him," Darrell said, nodding toward a young man with a badge on his blazer who strolled slowly through the gallery.

Dad went right over to the guard. "Excuse me. Is it possible to talk to a curator? We have a couple of questions about Ming artifacts."

The guard looked at his watch. "I think Dr. Powell is around this afternoon. Hold on." He went to a box on the wall, opened it, and pressed a few buttons on a keypad. He spoke into the receiver, listened for half a minute, then hung up. "She'll be right up."

"Thank you," said Dad. "That would be great."

But the moment I went for the tile in my pocket, Darrell snagged my sleeve. "Whoa, bro. We can't let anyone see the original. It's too valuable. Let's trace it instead. In the notebook."

"Good thinking," said Becca.

"Oh, I know," Darrell said, taking my notebook and a pencil from my bag and tracing the tile carefully on the page opposite my latest notes. He tore the page out.

"You're quite the artist," Becca told him.

"It's a gift I share with the world—"

"Hold on." Dad tugged us sharply behind a display of tapestries. "I just saw—"

"Leathercoat?" asked Lily.

"No, that acrobatic fellow from the airport," he

whispered. "The man who was making the baby laugh. Why would he be here?"

"At the same time we are?" whispered Becca. "Did he just see us?"

"I don't think so," Dad said as a young woman in a trim blue suit walked across the gallery toward us. "I'm going to find out what he's doing in the museum. Wait here with the curator. I'll be right back to talk with her." Dad slipped away from us and walked quickly to the end of the gallery, peeked around the opening, then slid into the next room and stepped slowly across the floorboards.

"Just like a secret agent," Darrell whispered. "Go, Dad."

I didn't like it. "Is this just random? The guy from the airport is suddenly where we are? Because I have to say, I don't think so."

"Your dad will figure it out," said Lily.

Becca raised her hand. "Here's the curator."

The young curator came over to us. Her name tag read *Tricia Powell*. "Was that your father I just saw?"

"He'll be right back," said Lily. "But we have some questions."

"Okay," she said brightly. "How can I help you until he returns?"

Everyone looked at me because I had the tracing in my hand.

"Um . . ."

"Yes?"

It was so hard to come up with an outright lie.

Not only hard to think up the words, but hard to say them to a stranger. I knew before the relic quest was over, I'd probably be much better at it than I ever wanted to be. But if a fib got us closer to a relic—and Sara—it was worth the risk.

"We found this drawing in my uncle's stuff when he died," I said, handing the tracing to the curator. "We wondered what it means. It looks sort of Chinese maybe, but we don't know for sure."

As she studied Darrell's suddenly awful tracing, I felt like a first grader trying to pull one over on his teacher. What I didn't expect was the look of total astonishment on her face.

"How did you get this?" she asked me.

"Um . . ."

"Like Wade said, it was in our uncle's stuff," Lily said.

"Uh, no," the curator said sharply. "And I didn't ask *where* you got this, I asked *how*. This is obviously not a drawing. It's a tracing. Did your uncle do this, or did you?"

She was smart. Knowing it was a tracing meant that she guessed we had access to the original.

"Uh . . ." I had nothing.

"Well, tell me, then, who exactly was your uncle?" she asked.

"A . . . collector," Becca said. Given Uncle Henry's antique-jammed Berlin apartment, that was not a lie at all. "He lived in Berlin, Germany. He died last week." Also not a lie.

"I'm sorry," the curator said. "Very sorry for your loss. But . . ." She shot a look at the security guard and frowned. "Follow me."

I glanced around. Dad wasn't anywhere in sight. I didn't want to leave the spot where he'd left us, but the curator walked only into the next gallery, so we followed.

She stood next to a tall display case housing four items on different levels. On the top sat a rectangular box about seven inches long by five inches wide and four or so inches deep. It was made of shiny ceramic. In the center of the lid were six round tiles and a gap where a seventh tile was missing.

The tiles were nearly identical to the tile in my pocket.

"You see?" Tricia Powell said. "Your tile appears very similar to the others in this piece—so similar, in fact, that I think I'll need to speak with your father about how you really came by this tracing."

We gaped like idiots until Becca pulled herself

together. "Can I ask you some questions first?" she said in her friendliest voice. "Then we'll tell you everything. Promise."

Tricia Powell folded her arms. "You know, I really should . . . but okay. You can ask me one question."

"One question?"

"One."

Becca swallowed. "Okay, here goes. *What* kind of box comes from *where* in China and was made *when* by *whom* to show designs that mean *what* . . . exactly?" She smiled hopefully at Dr. Powell.

Ha! I hoped the curator thought Becca as adorable as I did just then.

I guess she did, because she glared for a minute, then laughed despite herself. "Okay, that was one *really* long question! First, why don't you read the label, and we'll take it from there." She stepped back from the display case.

The label read:

Decorated Box
Chinese, Ming dynasty (1368–1644)
Early 16th century?

Porcelain with jade decorative tiles, featuring six of the seven "mansions" of the traditional Chinese astronomical

symbol known as 東方青龍, *or Seiryu, the Azure Dragon*
of the East, governing the season of Spring. Clockwise from
upper left are:

> *Virgo:* 角, *or Horn (Jiǎo), and* 亢, *or Neck (Kàng)*
>
> *Libra:* 氐, *or Root (Dǐ)*
>
> *Scorpio:* 房, *or Room (Fáng), and* 尾, *or Tail (Wěi);*
> *the tile representing* 心, *or Heart (Xīn), is missing*
>
> *Sagittarius:* 箕, *or Winnowing Basket (Jī).*
>
> *With yellow glaze and overglaze of green and white,*
> *and six of seven pale jade tiles embedded in the surface of*
> *the lid.*
>
> *Gift of Dolly and Alan Hughes (Hughes Collection)*
> *H1988.42.178b*

"There's a picture of the Hugheses in the brochure,"
Becca said, flipping it open for us to see. "So they gave
this box to the museum?"

"Among many other Ming pieces, nearly all from
the early to middle sixteenth century," said Dr. Powell.
"Alan Hughes was an early inventor of the technology that became the World Wide Web and was quite
wealthy. He died not long after he and his wife donated
this piece in 1988. His wife donated the rest of their collection in her will. She passed away three years ago."

"Do you know what's inside the box?" Lily asked.

"We've never been able to open it. We believe it

contains an internal lock that was broken over the last five hundred years. The artisans of the Ming court were among the most advanced in the arts and in mechanics, and we don't want to tamper with it. That's why the piece you . . . *traced* is so important. Some curators believe the box was used as a sort of sampler, to hold a variety of spices that traders would examine before buying and shipping to the West. But since we haven't opened the box, that's just a guess."

Like everything else about the Copernicus Legacy, this small box had just become infinitely more mysterious.

I really wanted Dad to hear what the curator was saying, but his tail on the guy from the plane must have taken him to some other part of the museum. "Dr. Powell, I know my dad will be back soon and have more questions, but is there any way we can get a closer look at the spice box?" I asked. "To see how the tracing fits with the rest of the design? It's hard to see through the glass."

Dr. Powell frowned. "I don't know." She checked the time on her cell phone. "We've been searching for the missing piece since we received the Hughes donation. And your tracing is so exciting. I'll be right back." She glanced at the guard and hurried out of the gallery.

It was actually kind of neat to see an adult so

enthusiastic about what a piece of paper could mean. Dr. Powell was definitely a geek, kinda like me. And Becca.

"I'm calling your dad; he needs to get back here," said Lily. She tapped in the number and put it on speaker. Dad picked up.

"I'm on the main floor," he said softly. "He's down here somewhere, but he's moving through the rooms quickly, so I'm not sure what he's doing." When we told him what the curator told us, he added, "What we don't want is to alert the police that we have something of Mr. Chen's. Say nothing. I'll find the director. Maybe it'll help that I have a bit of a name in science circles." He hung up.

"Cool dad, you guys," Lily said to Darrell and me.

"Do you think they'll want to buy my drawing?" Darrell asked.

"You mean your tracing?" I said.

"I'm thinking a sweet million for my artwork. Plus they name a gallery after me."

"Uh-huh," said Lily. "The Gallery of Wishful Thinking."

"Funny, people, really," said Becca, studying the spice box's label, "but Tricia Powell will be back soon. Lil, maybe you can take a picture of the box, and Wade, you could copy the label in your notebook."

We took photos and made notes. Before long, Dr. Powell was back. "I found your father with the director in her office. They're still chatting, but in the meantime she's agreed we can study the box in the conservation lab, so let's go."

Dr. Powell and the security guard unlocked the display case and removed the spice box—it was apparently heavier than it looked. We followed them into a large, well-lit room with an enormous worktable in the center and smaller desks around the edges. Scattered here and there were computers and devices, some of which looked like they belonged in a hospital emergency room. There was one person in a lab coat, bending over a magnifying glass. He talked briefly with Dr. Powell, then left with the guard.

She set down the spice box on one end of the white worktable. "Now, the tracing. May I?"

She made a photocopy of it and trimmed the extra paper away. Her fingers trembling slightly, she placed it gently over the box. She drew in a breath. "Wow. A perfect match. This is pretty amazing, I have to tell you. See how these strands of the design on your tile continue across the other six? What I wouldn't give to have the original." She gave us a quizzical look. "Excuse me for a second. I need to grab a couple of reference books. Please don't touch anything." She hurried out of the lab, and we were alone.

I knew I shouldn't have moved an inch, particularly after what my dad had said about not showing the original. But something came over me with the box just sitting there. At least I had to see the tile next to it. I fished it out of my pocket and held it over the gap in the box lid.

"Wade . . ." Becca lifted her hand to me, then stopped. "No, go ahead. Do it."

Darrell and Lily crowded on either side of us, breathless. The room went absolutely silent, like a vacuum. Like the cave in my dream. Trying to still my shaking fingers, I lowered the tile until it nearly touched the box. It slid down out of my fingers and dropped into place.

The moment I moved my hand away, the round jade tiles, all seven of them, began to turn.

CHAPTER ELEVEN

Each tile revolved in place as if on an invisible axis. A few went clockwise, others counterclockwise, some slowly, others more quickly, like seven dials seeking a single combination.

"Wade . . . Wade . . . ," Becca whispered. I didn't know what she meant by that, because she didn't say anything else. I wanted to answer, "Becca . . . Becca . . ." But I just looked up at her.

Then the box made a low grinding noise, like tumblers shifting.

Darrell shook his head. "Good-bye to the Darrell gallery. Dude, you just busted it."

"He didn't bust it," Lily hissed. Then she shot me a look. "Wade, you better not have."

One by one, the tiles stopped moving until only one—the slowest one, the one from Mr. Chen—was still spinning. Then it stopped, too.

So did the grinding. What had been a random collection of jade designs just moments before was now lined up in a single sequence across the top of the box. A complete picture emerged out of the threads of jade.

It was a scorpion.

"Scorpion, for Scorpio, the constellation?" asked Lily, without waiting for an answer. "And the relic! I know it's inside the box. This is what Leathercoat is looking for. We found another relic!"

Could we possibly have encountered a second relic so soon?

The answer was no. Seconds after the scorpion appeared in the design, the lid sprang open on invisible hinges, probably for the first time since the seventh tile was removed. The box was empty. Oddly, however, the inside of the box was coated with a layer of dull gray metal that I thought might be lead. That was what had made it heavy. The inside of the lid, also lead, had several lines of Chinese characters engraved on it.

Then the curator came back, toting a big pile of books.

She stopped in her tracks when she saw the spice box. "What in the world did you do?"

"We . . . ," I started. I took a deep breath before continuing. "We had the seventh tile, not just a tracing. I know we should have told you, and we're sorry. We can't really tell you how we got it, but it was given to us by a nice man who is now—"

"Out of town," Darrell said, jumping in.

"Do you have any papers?" Dr. Powell asked.

"Like our passports?" Lily asked.

"No, papers that document the tile," she said.

"No," I said, "but you can see it's not a fake. It's part of the original piece. See how it fits."

"Does your father know this?" she asked.

"He knows," said Becca. "That's probably what he's talking to your director about. He should be here very soon."

"The museum will want it, obviously," Dr. Powell said. "It's part of the spice box. But we can't acquire it if it doesn't have any documentation. And we'll likely have to call the police. I mean, I'm sorry, but the director is required to do that."

The enormous stupidity of what I'd just done was dawning on me. We could be in deep trouble. A priceless piece of art given to us by a murder victim? I should have let Dad handle it. Dumb. Dumb. Dumb.

"Excuse us a second, Dr. Powell. Guys . . ." Becca drew us back a few steps away from the table. "Look.

If this belonged to Mr. Chen, forgetting for a moment how *he* got it, wouldn't he have come here and done the same thing we just did? He had a piece of the puzzle leading to a relic—possibly Scorpio—and needed to attach it to the spice box. How would he have handled this situation?"

"There's no document somewhere deep in that pocket of yours?" Darrell asked me.

"I wish," I said. "Let's get Dad back here. Maybe we could donate the tile to the museum. I mean, just give it to them. Once we find out what it's supposed to tell us, we may not even need it anymore."

"It's worth a try," said Becca.

I flashed her a shy smile. "You say that now . . ."

We—I—told Dr. Powell what we'd decided and that she should talk to the director and my father, "who, by the way, is an astrophysicist at the University of Texas," which seemed to impress her. She was still suspicious, but the fact that we offered to donate the tile to the museum, and that my dad was making deals with the director, seemed to take some of the guilt away.

She said she would hold on to the tile until everything was decided. Which was fine with us. The tile seemed to be merely a way to open their spice box, and maybe the real clue was the writing inside.

"Um, if it's not too much to ask," said Lily, "do you

think you could translate the words on the inside of the lid?"

"What exactly are you working on?" Dr. Powell asked.

We shared a glance. "A legend," I said. "A story."

She seemed to accept that. "I'll translate the text for you. It will take me a few minutes." She sorted through the books she'd brought in and pulled down several more from a shelf and set them on the table next to her computer.

"Lily, you should probably take some pictures of this thing, right?" Darrell suggested.

Lily did. And so did Dr. Powell. She sent her photos to a computer sitting at the far end of the worktable so we could examine them in high resolution. We set ourselves up around it, while she turned her attention to the writing inside the box.

"This is definitely a Ming-era object," she said right off, "but the writing inside the lid is not Ming. Strange, no? The characters are modern simplified Chinese. This particular form of it wasn't even around until 1956 at the earliest."

"Dr. Powell, are you saying that writing was added to the box sometime in the last sixty years?" I asked.

She nodded once. "Yes. And please call me Tricia.

Now, come over here and look."

She moved the box under a lens that was connected to her computer. "There are two tiny impressions stamped into the inside of the lid. They *are* old." She pointed out a tiny ball with rings around it hovering over what looked like a small dish.

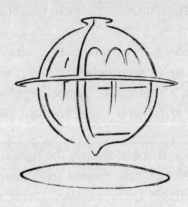

"It looks like a Christmas ornament," said Lily.

"Isn't it an armillary sphere?" I asked.

Tricia blinked. "It is! How did you know?"

"Wade's a geekologist at the University of Texas," said Darrell.

Actually, we all knew what it was. Copernicus's astrolabe had elements of a giant armillary sphere. There was a sketch of it in the diary, and we'd seen plenty of spheres at a museum on a hillside in Rome.

"Well, back when very few people knew how to read," Tricia continued, "images, drawings, and symbols were used to represent people or governments, rather than words."

"Like stained-glass windows for people who couldn't read Latin," Darrell said. "My mom taught me all about them."

Tricia nodded. "Absolutely. This armillary sphere is an image we've seen before in Ming work. It's not Chinese, but a Portuguese symbol representing King Manuel the First, who ruled Portugal from 1495 to 1521."

Becca glanced at me. Exactly the right time.

"The spice box was created in China. There's no doubt about that," Tricia went on. "From these marks I'd guess it was crafted in Beijing for either King Manuel or for a well-to-do Portuguese trader. Why it was lined in lead, I have no idea, but that seems original, too. Also, the little dish floating below the sphere could be the symbol of a specific merchant, but I'd have to do more research to track that down. This is so exciting! Now the text."

While Becca, Lily, and I went back to our computer and studied the images of the box, Darrell paced behind us. "We can't let on too much," he said, raising his eyes at the curator and keeping his voice low, "but here's what I think. Sometime in the past sixty years, a recent Guardian wrote the message in the spice box, then took out the tile to keep the box from being opened without it."

Lily's grin told us she liked the way that sounded. "But it wasn't just a spice box, was it? You wouldn't line it with lead if it only carried cinnamon. I'm thinking the relic used to be in here."

"Lead keeps Superman safe from Kryptonite," Darrell said, which seemed random, but it got me thinking.

"I wonder if you-know-who knew that in the 1500s."

"Unlikely," said Darrell. "The first Superman comic was in 1938."

I gave him a fake smile. "Not Superman. I mean if Copernicus knew that lead could protect you. When did people discover that?"

A hundred questions. No answers. Yet.

"Kids . . ." Tricia called us over. Everyone but Becca hurried to the other end of the table to see what she'd come up with. Becca leaned over the Copernicus diary, hiding it and reading intently, but gripping her arm tight, as if it was hurting all of a sudden. Lily shot me a worried look.

"The very first word of the text is on a line by itself, like a title," Tricia began, pointing to a series of three characters that looked like this: 壑融天. "It took me all this time to figure out because it's actually rendered backward, like a mirror image. Very strange. But once you reverse it, it's easily read as the Chinese character for the constellation Scorpio, which follows the scorpion design on the lid. Also, the lines below, though not backward, are a poem. I'll keep working."

At the other end of the table, Becca had her notebook out next to the newspaper-covered diary and was carefully unfolding the page that contained the Trithemius cipher.

"What did you find?" Darrell whispered to her.

"Remember how I showed you the line beginning one of the coded sections?" she asked. "'Bfe cyhylk bf wuxzz ifgb oiud and so on?"

"Ifgabood. I remember," said Darrell.

"Well, if this letter square is the way to decode it, maybe the key word is the title of the poem *Scorpio*, but not really *Scorpio*, but the reverse of it."

"You mean *oiprocs*?" Darrell said, almost without missing a beat.

"Uh . . . no," she said. "Not in English."

"Chinese?" said Lily. "No, the characters would be different."

Becca smiled, but her smile was strained as if even that hurt. "I'm thinking it could be Portuguese. Because of the markings Tricia found. I don't know Portuguese really at all, but maybe the computer—"

Lily's finger tapped on the museum's computer keyboard for a moment before she said, "*Scorpio* in Portuguese is *Escorpião.*"

"Go, Trithemius," I said.

Becca shook her head. "Not yet. It needs to be spelled backward, just like the symbol is in the box. So it's . . . *O-A-I-P-R-O-C-S-E.*"

"That's the key word?" I said.

"We'll see." Becca shifted over to the computer in front of Lily. "What we do is line up the letters of the key word above the coded word to give us the message in Portuguese. Like this." And she wrote out the key word— *OAIPROCSE*—over and over above the coded passage.

OAI PROCSE OA IPROC SEOA IPROCSEO
BFE CYHYLK BF WUXZZ IFGB OIUDQYKG

"The Trithemius cipher uses three steps," she went

on. "First you use the column of letters down the left side to locate the first letter of the key word. So, we see that *O* is about halfway down the left-hand column of letters."

Tabula tranfpolitionis auerfa.

```
w z y x u t s r q p o n m l k i h g f e d c b a
z y x u t s r q p o n m l k i h g f e d c b a w
y x u t s r q p o n m l k i h g f e d c b a w z
x u t s r q p o n m l k i h g f e d c b a w z y
u t s r q p o n m l k i h g f e d c b a w z y x
t s r q p o n m l k i h g f e d c b a w z y x u
s r q p o n m l k i h g f e d c b a w z y x u t
r q p o n m l k i h g f e d c b a w z y x u t s
q p o n m l k i h g f e d c b a w z y x u t s r
p o n m l k i h g f e d c b a w z y x u t s r q
o n m l k i h g f e d c b a w z y x u t s r q p
n m l k i h g f e d c b a w z y x u t s r q p o
m l k i h g f e d c b a w z y x u t s r q p o n
l k i h g f e d c b a w z y x u t s r q p o n m
k i h g f e d c b a w z y x u t s r q p o n m l
i h g f e d c b a w z y x u t s r q p o n m l k
h g f e d c b a w z y x u t s r q p o n m l k i
g f e d c b a w z y x u t s r q p o n m l k i h
f e d c b a w z y x u t s r q p o n m l k i h g
e d c b a w z y x u t s r q p o n m l k i h g f
d c b a w z y x u t s r q p o n m l k i h g f e
c b a w z y x u t s r q p o n m l k i h g f e d
b a w z y x u t s r q p o n m l k i h g f e d c
a w z y x u t s r q p o n m l k i h g f e d c b
```

"Step two is to locate the coded letter, in this case *B*, from *BFE*." Becca ran her finger from left to right along the row and stopped at *B*.

Tabula transpolitionis aucrfa.

```
w z y x u t s r q p o n m l k i h g f e d c b a
z y x u t s r q p o n m l k i h g f e d c b a w
y x u t s r q p o n m l k i h g f e d c b a w z
x u t s r q p o n m l k i h g f e d c b a w z y
u t s r q p o n m l k i h g f e d c b a w z y x
t s r q p o n m l k i h g f e d c b a w z y x u
s r q p o n m l k i h g f e d c b a w z y x u t
r q p o n m l k i h g f e d c b a w z y x u t s
q p o n m l k i h g f e d c b a w z y x u t s r
p o n m l k i h g f e d c b a w z y x u t s r q
o n m l k i h g f e d c b a w z y x u t s r q p
n m l k i h g f e d c b a w z y x u t s r q p o
m l k i h g f e d c b a w z y x u t s r q p o n
l k i h g f e d c b a w z y x u t s r q p o n m
k i h g f e d c b a w z y x u t s r q p o n m l
i h g f e d c b a w z y x u t s r q p o n m l k
h g f e d c b a w z y x u t s r q p o n m l k i
g f e d c b a w z y x u t s r q p o n m l k i h
f e d c b a w z y x u t s r q p o n m l k i h g
e d c b a w z y x u t s r q p o n m l k i h g f
d c b a w z y x u t s r q p o n m l k i h g f e
c b a w z y x u t s r q p o n m l k i h g f e d
b a w z y x u t s r q p o n m l k i h g f e d c
a w z y x u t s r q p o n m l k i h g f e d c b
```

"The final step is to follow *that* column all the way up to the top row of the square to give us the first letter of the message." Becca ran her finger up from *B* to the very top. It landed on *M*.

Tabula tranfpolitionis aucrfa.

```
w z y x u t s r q p o n (m) l k i h g f e d c b a
z y x u t s r q p o n m l k i h g f e d c b a w
y x u t s r q p o n m l k i h g f e d c b a w z
x u t s r q p o n m l k i h g f e d c b a w z y
u t s r q p o n m l k i h g f e d c b a w z y x
t s r q p o n m l k i h g f e d c b a w z y x u
s r q p o n m l k i h g f e d c b a w z y x u t
r q p o n m l k i h g f e d c b a w z y x u t s
q p o n m l k i h g f e d c b a w z y x u t s r
p o n m l k i h g f e d c b a w z y x u t s r q
(o) n m l k i h g f e d c (b) a w z y x u t s r q p
n m l k i h g f e d c b a w z y x u t s r q p o
m l k i h g f e d c b a w z y x u t s r q p o n
l k i h g f e d c b a w z y x u t s r q p o n m
k i h g f e d c b a w z y x u t s r q p o n m l
i h g f e d c b a w z y x u t s r q p o n m l k
h g f e d c b a w z y x u t s r q p o n m l k i
g f e d c b a w z y x u t s r q p o n m l k i h
f e d c b a w z y x u t s r q p o n m l k i h g
e d c b a w z y x u t s r q p o n m l k i h g f
d c b a w z y x u t s r q p o n m l k i h g f e
c b a w z y x u t s r q p o n m l k i h g f e d
b a w z y x u t s r q p o n m l k i h g f e d c
a w z y x u t s r q p o n m l k i h g f e d c b
```

"If I'm right," she said, "the message begins with the letter *M*."

She did the same with the second letter, going all the way down the left-hand column to row *A*, in to letter *F*, and up to letter *E*. The third letter—*I* to *E*—gave us *U*. The next word, *CYHYLK*, became *MESTRE*.

"Lily, anything?" asked Becca.

Lily searched the dictionary for the translation of the first two words. She jumped. "In Portuguese, *meu mestre* means . . . 'my master'!"

CHAPTER TWELVE

As Tricia Powell worked through her translation of the spice box poem at the other end of the table, Becca used the cipher square, the diary's coded passage, and the dictionary to translate the coded passage into her notebook. Then she whisper-read it so only we could hear.

My master has asked me to hide the words of this day, the xxii day of May 1514. . . .

It is past noon when the last gnarled branches fall away.

"Hans," he tells me, "we have found Ptolemy's lost ruins."

My heart stops to behold what is there in front of

us. It is clear, we have indeed found Ptolemy's secret.
In a deep pit amid the jungle-like growth in the
hidden depths of the island are the fragments of his
strange astral device.

    The base of the secret astrolabe.

    To be both as precise and as guarded as the
Magister has asked me to be, I will say that the
legendary Temple of ——— sits buried beneath a jagged
——— on the ——— side of the island, overlooking ———
to the sea.

    It is where the infamous guides assured us it could
never be.

    Master Nicolaus smiles. "Now begins the
reconstruction. For that, I must send for my brother."

"Whoa," Darrell breathed out. "That's the moment
they find Ptolemy's ancient astrolabe. This is incredible."
The diary had begun with Hans Novak's first entry
on February 13, 1514. Here it was, over three months
later, and they were on an island.

"Go on, Bec," Lily urged.

xxix June 1514
Nearly one month of weary toil has passed since
Nicolaus's brother arrived. Andreas looks like
Nicolaus enough to be his own double.

Then, something very strange.

This morning, Andreas emerges from the pit in which lies Ptolemy's device. His hands are bleeding. I run to get cloths.

"Brother," he says to Nicolaus, "the scorpion's tail may be long, but its claws slice like razors. I have lost much blood."

xvii July 1514

On the island still, the night as black as the pit wherein we discovered Ptolemy's device. In Frombork at this moment, so you will understand the hour, we would hear the vesper bells ring from the cathedral across from Nicolaus's tower.

After nearly three weeks, Andreas's wounds from the scorpion have not healed. His left hand, with which he is most adept, is black. His face has thinned and twisted even as the Magister and I hurry to complete the device before the change of days Ptolemy wrote of.

"The hours are running away," Andreas says, "and so is my time. I must seek a cure, if a cure may be found."

And thus, by boat, Andreas Copernicus leaves us this evening. "In my mind, Hans," says Nicolaus, "the

church bells toll with every splash of the oar that takes
my poor brother from me."

The centuries-old pages of the diary sat illuminated by the computer screen in front of Becca. Listening to the deep sorrow in the words she read, I was struck by how things so old can be as alive now as they were when they were first created.

Lily whispered what we all felt. "It's so amazingly sad. The Copernicus biography I read on the plane said that his brother died just a few years later than this. How terrible Nicolaus must have felt."

"I never knew his brother was involved in the building of the machine," I said. "The books say he had leprosy, but all this scorpion stuff, it makes me wonder . . ."

"He still doesn't tell us what island they're on," Darrell said. "It reminds me of those old charts showing dragons bobbing around in the sea. Maybe looking at old maps would help us figure it out."

"And what is the 'change of days'?" Lily asked. "'The change of days Ptolemy wrote about.' That sounds ominous."

It did sound ominous, as if there was suddenly a deadline we hadn't known about. "I wonder if Galina knows about a deadline for the astrolabe. Maybe that's why she's so obsessed with chasing down the relics. Is there any more?"

Becca frowned. "There's a teeny red drawing in the margin that is repeated next to another coded passage later in the diary. It's a scorpion, I think, but the key word we just found doesn't work for the later passage."

She showed us the margin.

Tricia suddenly stood at her table and stretched. "Kids? I translated the text inside the box. It's a poem. There's one odd thing I have to tell you about, but first listen to it."

Scorpio
The deadly claws of scorpion
Lie quiet in jade's green tomb.
Its guardian stands masked of face
And sinister of hand.
Seek him no more, no more
Upon this moving earth.

"Wow, thank you," said Darrell.

"Tomb guardians are common in Ming art," Tricia said. "As for the rest . . . well, I heard you talking before, so you might know better than I what it means. Is it really an old story you're working on?"

"Kind of," said Becca. "Kind of history, too. But I don't know if we actually *do* know any more. The poem seems like a riddle."

"Tricia, you said there was something else," I said.

The curator shifted her computer screen so we could see it. "See this symbol at the very end of the poem?" She zoomed in on an ink block made up of two more or less vertical lines, each with a top branch that nearly touched the other. Inside it were several smaller strokes and a dot in the upper right corner.

"What does it mean?" I asked.

"Well, that's just it," Tricia said. "This is not a Chinese character at all. It's not even ancient Chinese. I've emailed the image to my colleagues, but so far no one can identify it."

I looked into her eyes as she said that. I didn't know if I was getting better—or worse—at reading people, but if Tricia Powell was keeping something from us, she was very good at concealing it. She seemed to be telling us the absolute truth.

"Of course, it's modern, too," she said. "Not like the armillary sphere or the dish."

"Hmm. Excuse me for a second. . . ." Becca walked back to the table with the diary lying on it and sat right down.

"Thanks," I said to Dr. Powell, then joined the others at the table.

"Becca, you've just had a brainstorm," Lily whispered.

Becca smiled. "The dish. I just realized something. If the Guardian is a Portuguese trader from Lisbon, and the dish represents him or his name, maybe it's a clue to the last part of the scorpion story in the diary. Wade, your dad told us about that code in Berlin when we found the dagger. It's called a rebus, remember? Where a picture represents a word or a name. If the dish represents the trader's name and it gives us a word, we can translate the final part. Lily, back to the computer."

While Dr. Powell took more pictures of the spice box, Lily keyed in *plate* and *dish*, both of which translated into Portuguese as *prato*. The word meant nothing special and didn't make the code work.

"What's another word for what this looks like?" said Lily.

"*Platter?*" said Darrell. "*Saucer?*"

"It figures you'd know words that relate to food," said Lily. She keyed both words into the dictionary. "'Platter' is also *prato*, so no to 'platter.' Hold on. 'Saucer' is *pires*." She typed in a flurry of letters, hit Enter, and waited for the search response. Three or four entries down she hit a link. "Aha! Check this out. There was a Portuguese merchant named Tomé Pires, who lived from 1465 to either 1524 or 1540. He was a major trader between Europe and the Far East. He lived in China for many years and even died there."

"That's it! It has to be," said Becca. "Oh, please work. . . ."

She moved her fingers over the cipher square again, making notations in her notebook. It was coming. Words and sentences collected. This time, she was really zipping along.

Finally she put down her pencil. "Whoa . . ."

CHAPTER THIRTEEN

11 October 1518
Night. Cold stars. The streets of Lisbon lie over the next
hill.

    I rest at my campfire. By my side lies a thick cloth
woven of lead fibers, in which Scorpio sleeps.

    I know the properties of lead to shield oneself from
harm. But I have since learned of the legendary stone
called jade, found only in the distant East. Jade is said
to more strongly guard one from such dark energy as
our ancient Scorpio emits.

    And so I call upon a friend from days gone by—a
trader with the Chinese of the East. He will bring the
relic there and ask those Eastern artisans to craft for it
a shell of finest jade.

I glance up at the position of the stars over his city, and like clockwork, the branches rustle. My friend appears, carrying in his hands a simple lead casket that will soon, I hope, hold like a tomb the scorpion of Chinese jade.

"That's all," Becca said quietly. "The next coded part doesn't use this keyword. It must be about another relic and another Guardian."

I read the translation from her notebook again. "Copernicus had already hidden the Scorpio relic in lead," I said, "but he wanted it also sealed in jade. He was afraid of its . . . 'dark energy.' Guys, this sounds like some kind of radioactivity. But that can't be . . . can it?"

"Dad would know," said Darrell. "And Becca, you know I usually reserve praise for myself, and sometimes for Lily and Ifgabood over here, but that translation was awesome. My mom would totally agree."

We *were* good at figuring out stuff, but the mention of Sara and Dad made me realize that time was passing. We needed to put everything together, understand it, and get moving.

Tricia Powell received a phone call from her director. While she was talking, I quickly went over what we knew so far.

"Okay, look. In 1514, Copernicus and Hans Novak

leave Poland for some island. There they find Ptolemy's wrecked time machine. Copernicus sees how to fix it and really make it work. He calls his brother to help. Andreas comes, taking over some of the relics. One of them represents the Scorpio constellation. Only there's something weird about it. The claws are razor-sharp, and they poison him."

"Right," said Lily. "They all think it's leprosy, but it's not."

"It could be some kind of radium poisoning," I guessed. "Don't ask me how or why the relic got radio-active, but people at that time didn't know anything about radium. Leprosy was what people used to get back then, so they said Andreas had leprosy."

Becca nodded at that. "Fast-forward to when Copernicus decides to hide the relics. He remembers what he's heard about jade, this mysterious stone from the East. He thinks that jade can keep Scorpio from poisoning anyone else."

"Enter the trade guy, Tomé Pires, who meets Copernicus in Portugal," said Darrell. "He takes the scorpion in the lead box to China, where artists create a jade scorpion to hide it even better."

"Somehow, the original lead-lined box ends up here," I said. "But it's empty. So where's Scorpio now?"

Darrell's phone rang and he snapped it on speaker.

112

"Dad? Where are you? We're in the conservation center with the tile. We found out so much. Did you track down the baby-laughing man?"

"His name is Feng Yi," my dad whispered. "He was actually looking for us. Kids . . . he says he's a Guardian. He was working with Mr. Chen, and has information for us."

The hairs on the back of my neck bristled. I didn't know how to take this. A pair of Guardians?

"He came to warn us," Dad said. "There's a group working with the German. They're called . . . Star Warriors. I know it sounds crazy, but they're onto us now and they have razor weapons or something—"

There was a crash on the other end of the phone.

"Dad?" I said. "Dad!" The phone went dead.

Tricia Powell instantly ended her own call. "There's something going on downstairs. A security guard has been wounded. The museum is in lockdown!"

CHAPTER FOURTEEN

Chain walls fell quickly over the doors to the con-servation lab and hit the floor with a clank. Bolts slid instantly inside the door frames.

"Shh," Tricia said. I didn't hear anything except an alarm sounding on another floor, but she did. "Some-one's coming. . . ."

"Grab your stuff," Becca whispered, quickly gather-ing her notebook and the diary and shoving them into her bag. I wanted to take the box, or at least the tile, but Tricia stowed the mechanical box in a safe under one of the work counters. Then she pulled out a key card. Placing her finger on a pad and simultaneously sliding the card opened a locked door at the back of the room. "Everyone out, quietly."

She hustled us down a narrow hallway along the rear of the lab. It connected with a second hall that split off to both the front and the back of the building. A new alarm sounded from the direction we'd come from. "Is this about the 'story' you're working on?" she said, her face strained. When we didn't answer, she just said, "Follow me."

We'd gone through passages before, and I was sure we would again, but then we'd been escaping from the Order. Who was coming this time? Star Warriors? What in the world were they? More alarms started up, and we heard the sound of feet running behind us.

Tricia pushed on toward the end of the hall, where she unlocked the door with another fingerprint. It led into a small office. We paused for a moment to catch our breath, but my heart pounded so quickly I could barely get any air in my lungs.

Tricia's phone buzzed. "A text from the director. There are ten intruders, maybe more, some on each floor. The police are outside the building."

Another alarm sounded. "We have to get out of here," I said.

"Tricia, tell us where to go," said Becca.

The curator moved across the office to a back door. That required her key card, too. It led into a short passage, through another bolted door that she unlocked, and finally into a dim gallery. The chain wall closed behind us. There was a bank of shaded windows running along one side of the room, and I was stunned to see streetlights and car headlights blazing outside the museum. We had spent hours studying the box and translating the diary, and it was already evening.

As much as I wanted Dad to come for us, when I heard a small explosion behind us, I hoped even more that he was okay.

We hurried across the floorboards when there was a second muffled blast, and the chain wall blocking the entrance to the last gallery crashed to the floor. The opening darkened suddenly, and we crouched. But it was neither Leathercoat nor any alien star man. It was the guy Dad had told us about. The second Guardian. Feng Yi.

He approached us on tiptoe as if he was sliding across the floor. His slender finger was at his lips. "Children, your father sent me. Tell me yes or no. Do you have the scorpion box with you?"

Tricia gave him a worried look. "It's in the safe."

Feng Yi nodded once. "Good. Markus Wolff has sent the Star Warriors for it, but you have foiled them for now. Please follow me—"

Before we could move or ask who Markus was, a bunch of figures in sleek black jumpsuits flew into the room, completely blocking the exit. Their heads and faces were obscured by scarves, their hands by black gloves. Then we heard the sound of clinking metal as they lunged forward.

"Throwing stars! Down!" Feng Yi shouted. We hit the floor as tiny sparks of light whooshed across the room at us. Glass shattered all around, setting off more alarms.

"Are you hurt?" Feng Yi whispered, his cheek red and wet.

"No, but—" Tricia started as he crept away, and more glittering flashes—stars with razor-sharp edges—ripped across the open space, clattering to the floorboards amid the broken glass and shards of ancient pottery.

The black-clad men raised their hands. "Come out," one said.

"Stop! Please stop!" Tricia cried.

The metal stars flew at the sound of her voice. Glass exploded on the far side of the room. Tricia dropped to the floor unhurt, then rolled behind the display case near Darrell and Lily.

"Give us what we want," the Star Warrior said in robotic English.

Meanwhile, Feng Yi had slithered across the floor like a snake, and he now emerged behind the bulk of the black-uniformed warriors.

As if he were on springs, he leaped up. With a series of amazingly high jumps across the room—half circus act, half martial arts movie—he tossed his own gold stars like a machine gun. Most of the scarfed men scattered for cover, but three went ahead and charged us.

Feng Yi shot more metal stars. The three fell back, groaning. "Dr. Powell," he yelled, "take them out of here now!"

She rushed ahead, unlocking the far door and shouting into her phone, while Darrell and Lily bounced to their feet and hurried after her.

"Becca, let's go!" I slung her bag over my shoulder and pulled her up by the hand of her good arm.

Feng Yi threw himself between us and the men, hurling another barrage at the attackers, and we raced out of the dark room to the clatter of metal stars.

CHAPTER FIFTEEN

Tricia hurried Lily and Darrell down a silver-walled hallway. Becca and I ran to catch up. Suddenly the yells from the gallery behind us stopped.

Darrell blew out a breath. "Oh, no, they got him. . . ."

There was the thump of another muffled blast; then Feng Yi jogged down the hall toward us, trailing a cloud of white. "A smoke bomb will confuse them," he said. "Ah, look down there—" He pointed out the windows. My dad was on the sidewalk below, speaking with a suited woman who I assumed was the museum director. Then he hurried off down the street, looking back over his shoulder at the museum.

"Sometimes the best offense is a hasty retreat," Feng Yi said. "Please come with me. I have told your father of a safe place. I will take you there now. But we must move quickly!"

Becca slid her hand from mine. I hadn't realized I was still holding it. "Is your dad really all right with this?" she whispered.

"We sort of have to trust that he is," I said under my breath. "He said so on the phone. Let's do what this guy says, but be careful."

We hurried along the windows to another room that opened onto a landing. A squad of police officers raced up the stairs toward us.

"In the main gallery," Tricia said to them, pointing.

"Clear the building," one of the officers instructed as the squad moved up past us, guns drawn. Alarms were going off all over.

When we reached the bottom of the stairs, another group of policemen led us out the front doors together. Dr. Powell turned to us, wrapping her arms around herself. It was cold with the sun down. "This whole thing is horrifying," she said, breathing hard. "Your father . . . I'm going to ask the director what in the world is going on."

"I will guard them from here," Feng Yi said to her with a nod. "Their father, Dr. Kaplan, is awaiting them. Children, come."

And that was it. We left Tricia Powell openmouthed

on the steps and rushed down the stairs after Feng Yi. Was this our new life? Living in the center of a hurricane? The Star Warriors were still in the building, and several late-working museum employees were still streaming out. The police didn't make any motions to speak with us. I wouldn't have known what to say to them anyway. It was a good time to slip away, so we did.

"We have not been properly introduced," the man said, trotting quickly down the sidewalk away from the stairs. "As your father told you, Feng Yi is my name. I am—was—working with Mr. Chen. I knew the museum was to be our first stop. When I saw your father in the gallery and remembered him from the plane, I instantly assumed that Mr. Chen had passed over the tile to you. Then we saw the Star Warriors together, and I hurried to find you."

"How did you know?" I asked. "About us, I mean?"

He turned toward me as we reached the corner. "How does one Guardian know another?" He smiled calmly, despite the fact that his chest was heaving. "Your father gave me this note to assure you. My limousine awaits. No more questions just yet. All will be revealed!"

I took it from him as we hurried across the street against the light.

*Feng Yi will protect you. He has
information for us. I'll meet you at
his restaurant. Be safe.*
—Dad

It was Dad's familiar scribble. I passed it to Darrell.

"You have a restaurant?" Darrell asked. "What kind of restaurant are we talking about? Never mind; I don't care. I'm starving!"

"We all are," said Becca, who was holding her arm now. She must have reinjured it during the attack, so it was a good thing I was carrying her bag.

"You need to rest," I said.

"I'm fine, Wade." She smiled at whatever my face was doing. "Really. I'll tell you when I'm not." Her smile faded away.

"A trusted friend works at the Red Dragon, a dim sum house in Chinatown," Feng Yi said over his shoulder. "In his back room we may enjoy privacy. Neither Markus Wolff nor his soldiers will find it."

"Markus Wolff," I said. "Tall guy with white hair. Long leather coat?"

"The very same," said Feng Yi

"So Leathercoat's name is Markus Wolff," said Lily. "And those guys work for him? He seems like such a loner."

He smiled. "They do work for him. The Teutonic Order employs all sorts of men—and women—to achieve their ends. As you know too well, they will stop at nothing to obtain every single relic of Copernicus's astrolabe from its hiding place."

The mention of Copernicus zinged through me. I thought of the cave. And Becca in my dream, and here and now. And I thought of Sara. I wondered where exactly we were on the path to finding her.

Feng Yi smiled thinly as he popped open one of the limousine's doors. "Your father will be very happy to see you. Take a seat."

It was happening so quickly—discovering the tile, translating the diary, the legend of the Scorpio relic, the attack by star-wielding ghosts, and now this, sitting in a comfortable limousine on the way to a restaurant? To say nothing of where Leathercoat—Markus Wolff—was in all of this. Very near, I guessed, and yet invisible.

Almost the entire car ride, Feng Yi was on his phone. Finally, he closed it. "The Star Warriors have vanished like shadows from the museum, which was only to be expected. They were gone before the police arrived in the upper gallery."

"Who exactly are they?" asked Becca.

Feng Yi breathed in and out slowly. "Centuries ago, a group of legendary fighters called themselves the Star

Warriors. They protected the emperor of China on his travels, using nothing but throwing stars. The Teutonic Order—Galina Krause—has somehow resurrected the ancient league of fighters to use as her agents in the Far East. They work for Markus Wolff now."

"You use throwing stars, too," said Darrell.

"The Star Warriors were onto something," Feng Yi said. "The Ming court was known for the ingenuity of its hidden weapons. When thrown properly, these stars are perfectly balanced to achieve high velocity and deadly accuracy."

"Do you always have them with you?" I asked.

The limousine wove down a crowded street of small boutiques and food shops. The air was thick with the noise of people, and the store windows were lit up and welcoming. "Even under my pillow," he said. "The life of a Guardian, as you are learning, is one of extreme and constant danger."

Eighteen minutes later, we reached San Francisco's Chinatown. The limo stopped outside a giant three-roofed arch shaped like a big green pagoda, and the car doors opened a moment later. The street rising beyond the arch glowed with colored lights. The sky above was already a deep blue.

"Follow," Mr. Feng said as he strode confidently

under the arch. "My friend knows we're coming. Your father is waiting for us there."

Glancing at the others, I saw everyone seeming a bit more at ease now. Alert, but not alarmed. I felt the same. Becca's arm didn't seem to be hurting right then, either, because she was walking freely, looking at all the food shops, clothing stalls, and lantern-lit temples on both sides of the street. My attention turned to our rescuer.

Feng Yi was probably in his forties, a few inches taller than my father, slim and muscular, with a broad back and long, slender hands—very like an acrobat or dancer. His face was angular, chiseled. He had a broad square jaw, and a faint scar where the cleft of his chin would be. Maybe the most striking thing about him was the mane of jet-black hair that fell to his shoulders. He walked with purpose and ease, like an athlete. Like Darrell, actually, who was a few steps back from Mr. Feng.

The streets were narrow and packed, which strangely made me feel safer than somewhere less populated, but our trek to the Red Dragon didn't take long. Mr. Feng stopped at a narrow red building with gold doors. A green-and-gold pagoda-shaped roof of several stories was perched above the neighboring building, which might have been a temple. Even before he opened the door, the spicy smells from inside the restaurant blossomed all around us, and I practically screamed from hunger.

The dim sum house was small but lavishly decorated with red lanterns and wall hangings covered in gold Chinese characters. The tables were close together and elegantly covered in white tablecloths with red napkins and flickering red lanterns. The main room was packed with chattering tourists as well as casual locals and their families. Darrell checked his watch and showed me. It was just after eight p.m.

I scanned the room. "I don't see Dad," I said suspiciously.

"Your father is in the back. Come," said Feng Yi. "Please."

We followed Feng Yi cautiously through a beaded curtain into a short hallway. At the end was a plain door with a dragon painted in red on it. Feng Yi opened it, and I have to admit that I cringed a tiny bit when he did. There was no need. On the other side of the door was a small, private dining room decorated much like the front room, except that it held a single large table, with a red tablecloth instead of white.

Dad was sitting at it.

Even before he bolted to his feet, we were all mashed up in a group hug.

CHAPTER SIXTEEN

"Please, have a seat." Feng Yi said this softly and easily, as if he hadn't just fought off a small army in the last half hour. "My friend Liang will bring us food and drink."

I'd been so happy to see my dad, I hadn't noticed the other man enter the room behind us. He was tall and thin like Mr. Feng, and wore the white uniform of a chef. He set down a pitcher of water, smiled at each of us, then disappeared through a swinging door.

When he did, the kitchen aroma wafted in. I think I drooled. At least, my stomach gurgled, which I didn't think anyone heard, until Darrell laughed; then everyone did.

"We may speak freely," Feng Yi assured us as we

settled in. "I trust Liang utterly. He has been my friend and associate for decades."

"I can't thank you enough, Mr. Feng—*we* can't thank you enough," Dad said. "Without your help, I don't know where we'd be right now." He smiled around at Darrell and me and the girls. "Not safe, for sure."

Mr. Feng rose to pour water in our glasses. "The term *Guardian* is many leveled," he said. "Helping our own is part of our creed, binding us to one another and to our mission. Now, let us share information."

I wanted to brush all my caution out of the way, especially since we were finally together again—and food was on the way—but it wouldn't leave me. The way Feng Yi had swept in to rescue Dad and us was awesome, and a real spectacle. I was grateful, really. But it was also . . . convenient. I wasn't sure how much Guardians knew about us, but asking him questions might tell us.

"Mr. Feng," I started, "can I ask you something?"

"By all means."

Dad fixed his eyes on me and nodded to go ahead. "Markus Wolff, the German man, he's not here for . . ." I stopped. "I mean . . ."

"For Vela, is this what you mean?" he said.

So he knew about Vela, at least.

"All of what the Order does is about every one of the twelve relics of the Copernicus time machine," he said.

"They are linked in different ways. You must know that the symbol of the Teutonic Order is the kraken?"

Of course we knew that. Uncle Henry's first coded message used the word before we discovered what it really meant. Hearing it again made me uneasy all over again. I nodded.

"Well, Markus Wolff and his Star Warriors are arms of that great kraken whose head is Galina Krause herself. They are her servants. Often they are slaves of the Teutonic Order. Allow me to show you."

From a locked cabinet on the wall next to the kitchen, he removed a black leather satchel. "Do you recognize this?"

We didn't, although the black leather was the same as Wolff's coat.

"I stole it earlier from Herr Wolff, and Liang has kindly kept it for me here. One compartment is locked by a clever microchip device, the sort that will destroy its contents—and its carrier—if it is breached. But this will interest you." From another compartment, he slid out a tablet computer of a sort I'd never seen before. It was compact, black, and rugged.

"We could sure use one of those," said Lily, practically sitting on her hands to keep from snatching it out of the man's grasp.

"Is that Leathercoat's?" Darrell asked.

Mr. Feng smiled at the name. "It is. I have friends—Guardians—in Shanghai who work in the Chinese government computer surveillance division. They are seeking a way to unlock the compartment, but in the meantime, they have reconstructed Wolff's last conversation on this tablet. Behold . . ."

He tapped the power switch and held the tablet so we could all see the screen. A few moments later, it lit up with the image of a ghostly white face surrounded by jet-black hair.

It was the face of Galina Krause.

As close to us as if she were in the room.

CHAPTER SEVENTEEN

Galina Krause was nearly as hypnotic on the tablet's screen as she is in real life. *Beautiful* doesn't even begin to describe her—with her two differently colored eyes, her skin as white as snow, and her raven hair (about which, by the way, don't get Darrell started, at least not in front of Lily).

We had seen her several times, but never so close as in that cave in Guam, where she had demanded we give Vela to her. When we refused, Galina shot her crossbow at us, wounding Becca, who now winced to see the woman's face, and it made me angry all over again.

After a quick rattle of words in German, we heard the off-screen voice of Markus Wolff speak to Galina in

English. "I am sending several images to the Copernicus servers in Madrid."

"Madrid?" said Darrell. "Is that where they plan to take Mom . . . ?"

Dad was riveted on the image. "That may be a lead."

I realized at that moment what he'd meant in Honolulu about the Copernicus servers and the Order's vast computing resources.

Galina smiled coldly into the screen. "So the great Markus Wolff requires the resources of our databases?"

"For analysis only." Several pictures shot down the left side of the screen. Pictures of us in the Honolulu airport, of Mr. Chen, of the phone store where Dad bought the new phones, and finally of the Asian Art Museum. "I believe they have deposited their valuables under lock and key," he said. "They do not act as if they are in possession of them."

"So he doesn't know where they are," said Lily under her breath. "Good."

"They will retrieve them before their next flight," said a tinny voice.

Ebner von Braun, Galina's creepy little troll assistant, now appeared on-screen. The forehead wound Uncle Henry had given him before he was murdered was finally starting to fade. "We will monitor storage facilities in the area," he said, "and alert you as to their vulnerability."

Feng Yi paused the video and turned to Dad. "Perhaps you will want to share this information with me. I can easily have armed guards assembled to keep your things safe. Should you need them."

I glanced at my dad. He was frowning. "I don't think we will. But thank you." When the video resumed, Galina was back on-screen, her lips redder than before, as if she'd just snacked on something living. "Are the legends true? You are close to the true Chinese relic?"

"One of the scorpions traveled here to California some years ago," Wolff said. "Our friends in Hong Kong think it is genuine, too."

"And the target?" she asked.

The word was terrifying. More so because she said it so casually.

"Targets," he said, emphasizing the plural. "One has already met his ancestors." He obviously meant Mr. Chen.

"Have you the resources you need?" Galina asked.

"You know I do. And after this?"

"Wait for my orders. Do not leave empty-handed."

"Have I ever?" The image of Galina Krause vanished, and the screen went black. That was it.

"So you see," Mr. Feng said, returning the tablet to the black bag, "you are up against the full resources of the Teutonic Order. You have unwittingly entered a war beyond your comprehension. The Star Warriors are but one faction in this war. What you know can help us."

The way he expressed himself was measured and correct, perfectly fluent in English words and phrases, though it was also clear from his accent that English was not his first language. I found myself wanting to steer the conversation away from secrets, but I couldn't find a way to do it that didn't seem obvious. So I turned to my dad, as if I'd just remembered something personal.

"Oh, Dad, I have to ask you something. . . ."

I stood up, and we crossed the room together. Out of the corner of my eye I watched Feng Yi's expression, to see if our move was suspicious to him, but he wasn't looking at us. All his attention seemed to be on Liang, who'd just come in, rolling a cart of fragrant dumplings, salads, soups, and bowls of things that smelled awesome.

"Dad," I whispered, "is he okay? I mean, legit? It's like he popped up out of nowhere, right where we happen to be, and suddenly he's rescuing us. I mean . . ."

Being almost as sneaky as I was, Dad smiled calmly in case Feng Yi was looking. "I know what you mean. He did help me get clear of Wolff's soldiers. If he weren't a Guardian, you'd have to wonder why he'd do that, right? And he helped you, Darrell, and the girls escape."

"Yeah, he did," I said. "His fight with the Star Warriors was epic. Flying through the air, throwing stars, and all. Maybe I'm too suspicious."

"No, just suspicious enough," he said. "Be cautious. That's the only way." He took his glasses off and rubbed his eyes. He looked tired.

"Any news on Sara?" I asked.

He tilted his head one way, then the other, and then put his glasses back on. "I almost don't want to say, but I spoke with the Bolivian investigator on the way here. Things are moving. Cross your fingers—I think we'll have a good answer, and it might be soon." He put his arm around me—whether to assure me or himself, I didn't know. "But everything we learn here will help."

"Like that Galina's in Madrid, maybe?" I said.

He nodded. "If we all keep alert, listen, and stay careful."

When we rejoined the others, Lily said, "You have to hear this—"

Darrell cut her off. "Before you do, eat this. I have no idea what it is, but you need to have some." He handed me a bowl of steaming blobs drenched in gravy. "Seriously. These dumplings are amazing."

I tried one. "Wow," I said, swallowing. "So good . . ."

Lily glared at us. Then she turned to Feng Yi. "Mr.

Feng, please excuse them. A few of us don't get out much. Can you say all that again?"

Mr. Feng grinned and bowed his head. "Some of this you already know. Years ago, one of the twelve relics—an iron scorpion, representing the constellation you call Scorpio—made its way in a box lined with lead to the capital of China. Once there, the scorpion, which Copernicus believed was deadly, was sealed in an outer body of the finest jade."

"Which is now in San Francisco," I said.

"Which is *perhaps* in San Francisco," Mr. Feng said. "You see, the Ming artisans created not *one* jade scorpion, but *five*. One for the true relic, and four slightly different scorpions as decoys. Each of the five jade figurines was given its own identical mechanical box."

"Whoa, we didn't know that," I said, glancing at the others.

Becca raised her eyebrows at me. "Right?"

"Thus, while each outer box is the same, tiny markings on the four decoys themselves lead to the true relic, as, in fact, the twelve relics lead to one another," Feng Yi continued. "All five scorpions remained in the vaults of the Forbidden City for nearly five centuries. Until thirty years ago, when a thief broke in and stole them—all five of them. Because the Order was just as frantic to locate them, the Guardians were convinced that the thief was, in fact, *not* a Knight of the Teutonic Order.

"Remember now, only one of the five jade scorpions contained the original relic of Copernicus's astrolabe. Unless a person uncovers a clue left by Copernicus himself, there appears to be no way to tell the five figurines apart. When I rose up in the ranks of the Eastern Guardians, I worked with Mr. Chen to locate the true Scorpio relic and bring it safely back to Beijing. Over the years we have located three. All three were beautifully constructed decoys. But Mr. Chen happily located a tile to a fourth box. Our experts have read the markings on the decoys, and I am nearly certain the true relic is here in San Francisco. Markus Wolff, who is no fool, believes it also."

We sat there, mesmerized, trying to take it all in, adding this to what we'd learned from the spice box. The poem inside it was still a mystery, and I really didn't want to share it, but I thought Mr. Feng could at least shed some light on the strange non-Chinese character at the end. Could I trust him enough to let him see it?

"So the German man is working with the Star Warriors," said Becca. "Is that because of the China connection?"

Mr. Feng's lips were set in a grim smile. "Exactly so. He recruited them in Beijing. You see, Wolff is like his name: a fearless, relentless hunter. He will use any means possible to find the relics for Galina. Alas, because Vela has crossed paths with Scorpio in this very city, Wolff now hopes to obtain both with a single move. You are his target now. Perhaps it is good luck that we, too, have crossed paths at this same moment, yes?"

Luck? I didn't believe in luck anymore, good or bad. Nothing was a coincidence where the Copernicus Legacy was concerned. Nothing.

"Can I ask why you don't know your fellow Guardian in San Francisco?" Dad asked.

Mr. Feng breathed out a long breath. "After the passing of your friend Heinrich Vogel—Uncle Henry, to you children—the Guardians' communications network was broken. For good reason."

"I understand," my dad said. "But how can we find the relic now?"

"We . . . ?" Mr. Feng ran a slow hand over his long hair and brought it back to rest on the table in front of him. "Dr. Kaplan, you are in the center of a war. In the trenches, so to speak. Do you want to be here? I suggest you do not. You have your family with you. So that we Guardians may do *our* job, the task that centuries have prepared us for, perhaps you can tell me what you have discovered. If, for example, you have some Chinese script, I can decipher it for you. . . ."

138

It was the gentlest way I'd ever heard of saying *Tell me everything you know; then go away.*

I glanced up at my dad to see how he'd take this. He smiled, like he had when we were talking across the room. For some reason, Becca had been watching the two of us. Maybe because she was smart and could "read" people and thought through stuff before she said it, she seemed to catch on to our caution. Before anyone could say anything, she turned to Lily. "Inside the spice box there was a character. Dr. Powell from the museum said she couldn't identify it. Maybe you can, Mr. Feng. Lily, the photo of the symbol?"

"I made it my wallpaper, plus there's the spice box and the poem you can help with," she said, opening her phone, but Becca snatched it gently away before she could show Mr. Feng anything.

"Ah, you have the images of the spice box here, do you?" Mr. Feng said, leaning over as Becca enlarged the image of the non-Chinese character for him.

He studied it, taking in every detail of the brush strokes.

"I am surprised, or perhaps not so surprised," he said. "Dr. Powell certainly knows the peculiarities of Ming court dialects. I must assume she was lying to protect the relic. The Order reaches everywhere."

Becca frowned at the warning. She liked Tricia—we all did. Certainly the young, friendly curator hadn't seemed to be lying.

"Do you know what the symbol means?" Lily asked, reaching for the phone, which Becca wouldn't release.

Mr. Feng traced his fingers slowly in the air. "It is the character called *fēng huǒ tái*. It means, 'tower with beacon.' There are many towers in San Francisco, some skyscrapers, but fewer with beacons atop them. Guardians have a deep sense of tradition. I believe the character is pointing us to an older tower. Such as the tower on Telegraph Hill. It is called Coit Tower."

"Do you think the relic is hidden there?" Darrell asked.

"It is indeed possible. You may leave your things here while we have a look. My limousine should be close by—"

We heard a sudden crash from the front of the restaurant. Customers shrieked. A table went over; dishes shattered. Liang rushed into the room, his face dark with fear. He uttered some quick words to Mr. Feng, who jumped to his feet, throwing stars in his hands.

"The Star Warriors! They have found us!"

CHAPTER EIGHTEEN

"**I** should have known!" Feng Yi snarled, leaping up from the table. "Wolff's bag must contain a GPS microchip. Everyone down—"

We heard the Star Warriors barreling through the tables in the dining room, but there was no time to escape. We hit the floor as they tore the door from its hinges and pushed Liang roughly to the wall.

Feng Yi crouched and scattered a handful of throwing stars over our heads. Several of the black-clad warriors fell to their knees screaming, clutching their sudden wounds. One spat words in Chinese at Mr. Feng.

"Never!" he cried, and a second round of stars flew. The warriors retreated back into the restaurant's main room and shot their weapons from there. Plaster and glass exploded behind us.

I felt a rush of cool air from outside as the diners fled the restaurant.

"Hurry! Out!" Liang yelled, his first words in English, as he pulled a pistol from inside his chef's uniform and shot at the attackers.

Dad snagged our bags and pushed the girls through the swinging door Liang held open, then tugged us into the steamy kitchen with him. I looked at Lily, who was staring wide-eyed at Feng Yi, whose hand was bleeding. The cooks shielded themselves behind the counters and on the floor. Feng Yi managed to fling more stars back through the door before it swung closed. Liang, firing occasional pistol shots, slipped in behind us.

"Quickly now," Feng Yi shouted. He and several of the cooks pushed a massive, industrial-size refrigerator in front of the door. "This will only give us a few minutes. Follow me."

He hurried us out of the kitchen into an alleyway outside. The sky was blue-black now, and the streetlights and store signs spotted the alley with deep shadows. We started toward the street, but several men blocked the way and ran toward us.

"This way!" Feng Yi yelled. He pulled down a fire

escape ladder from the wall behind us, and we scrambled up as fast as we could. "The roof connects to the temple next door. We can elude Wolff's men and escape through the pagoda."

We followed Feng onto the roof—Lily first, then Becca, then Dad, me, and Darrell. One by one, we were out and running breathlessly across the roof, which was flat except for the multiroofed pagoda straddling the temple. "This way!" Feng Yi called as he bounded across the roof, looking back over his shoulder at the fire escape stairs. I shot a glance at Darrell. His forehead was bright with sweat, his eyes wide.

Dad, Lily, and Becca had already disappeared through the pagoda's small doorway. Darrell and I tried to follow, but we were suddenly cut off by a rain of throwing stars from Wolff's men, who were swinging up the stairs and onto the top of the building. Their stars tore up the roof in front of us. There was nowhere to go. We froze where we stood. The terrifying men advanced slowly. I looked around. Feng Yi was nowhere to be seen. Dad, Becca, and Lily were inside the pagoda, probably racing down to the street and safety without realizing we weren't right behind them.

The Star Warriors spread out with a series of identical moves, like a line of robot killers doing a ballet. We backed up until we couldn't.

Darrell groaned under his breath. "I don't like our options."

"We have options?"

"One," he said, "and I guess if you only have one, it's not really an option, but it sounds more hopeful to say it that way—"

"Are you still talking?"

Someone barked a command, and the men charged—then immediately started collapsing in groans. Throwing stars showered down on them from above like a monsoon in Guam.

"Yes!" I crowed, then suddenly felt an ironlike grip on my forearm. It was Feng. His hand was like a winch, dragging me up to the lowest of the pagoda's three roofs even as he kept hurling stars at the men. They split apart, then tried to regroup. After I was safe on the landing reshouldering my bag, which had slipped down my arm, he reached for Darrell and swung him up with ease. We rushed around to the far corner of the sloping roof, away from the Warriors.

"We ascend one more roof to another entry inside," Feng whispered, digging his hands into his pockets for more stars.

Darrell and I were safely out of range when there came a single gunshot from the direction of Wolff's men. After the delicate tinkling of metal stars, it sounded like an explosion, smashing into the pagoda tiles behind us. Mr. Feng cried out; his pant leg was slashed and bloodied. He fell awkwardly and slid down the tiles, grasping wildly for something to hold on to. Wolff's bag slid from his shoulder and flew out away from him, as if it was going to tumble down into the street below.

I threw my bag off, flattened on the roof, and reached for him. But I only managed to snag the strap of his black satchel. I tried to hoist it back over my shoulder to free my hand, but the bag was heavy. I started to slip. "Darrell!"

I pedaled my feet on the slick roof tiles, desperate not to slip off. There was another muffled shot, and Mr. Feng howled in pain. I reached out as far I could, but he was sliding too fast.

"Help!" he cried. "Help!"

Darrell's grip was on me like a vise. I swung out with my free hand but managed only to graze Mr. Feng's fingertips.

The man dropped suddenly to the roof below, rolled once to the edge, and disappeared over the side.

CHAPTER NINETEEN

I yelled. I must have yelled. Air rushed from my throat, but all I heard was Feng's scream—a long fiery echo that drove into my ears like a hot dagger. Then it ended, and traffic, car horns, music roared like a waterfall. I tried to look over the side, but Darrell, braced flat on the lip of the roof, had his hands clamped on my wrist.

"Don't dangle, you dope!"

He reached behind him, took hold of a railing, and pulled me. I was able to swing my foot higher, then higher, until it caught the ledge, and he dragged me back onto the pagoda roof.

"Come on," he growled. "We have to get out of here."

I crawled after him through a small door in the center of the pagoda and slid down to the floor inside.

Someone was blubbering. Maybe it was me? Yeah, definitely me. Darrell couldn't get a word in.

Besides the waterfall in my ears, I was actually wet. My shirt was once again soaked with sweat. Darrell clamped his arm tight around my shoulder and led me to the stairs. We stumbled down through the temple to street level. Dad and the others rushed over to us, but there wasn't time to talk. He took charge right away, drawing us into the alley again. Or was it a different alley? I wasn't sure. I just had to follow him. Becca was on one side of me, Darrell on the other. Dad and Lily led the way.

After a while, the open sky was above us. We were in a park, next to a tall building, and there were redwood trees all around. It was nearly completely dark by now. I wasn't sure how we'd gotten there, or if the star throwers had followed us. I was shivering with fear and cold.

"He's dead," I said. "Feng Yi is dead. I couldn't hold on to him."

"Wade, look at me," my father said, his voice very calm and comforting. "Wade, listen. Maybe he's not dead. Maybe he . . . landed somehow. He's an acrobat, remember. And there would be sirens."

And then there were sirens, winding closer on the crowded streets behind us. Still quaking, I focused on

Dad's face. It was growing very dark behind him, like the sun had set all over again. Dark as night, like the cave at the end of my dream. Then his face was dark, too.

Then I passed out.

I woke up two or three minutes later. We were in the same park as before, only this time I was lying on the ground under one of the thick-trunked trees. Dad, Darrell, Becca, and Lily were all around me, like that scene in *The Wizard of Oz* where Dorothy wakes up and realizes it was all a dream.

Except it wasn't.

"You went out like a light," Darrell said. "*Click*. First you were there; then you weren't. I thought you died. We all thought you died. But you didn't, because you opened your eyes just now, which is a good sign. I'm just saying. If you think you're dead, you aren't."

"Darrell," Dad said. "Give him some space."

I breathed in. Lily pulled a plastic water bottle out of her bag and held it in front of my face. I sat up, leaned against the tree, and drank until I couldn't anymore.

Becca sat on a stone bench facing me, but she kept glancing nervously over her shoulder. She wore a crazy scared sort of . . . what? Smile? Maybe because I was still alive, or maybe because she was in shock, like me, and couldn't make her face do any other expression.

My fingers were sore. I realized they were still clenched tightly around the straps of Markus Wolff's black satchel, while Darrell had snagged mine from the pagoda roof. Lily slipped the satchel off my arm and set it on the bench next to Becca.

"Where are we?" I asked.

"A place called Bierman Park," Dad said. "I remembered it from when Sara and I were here. We're out of Chinatown, a few blocks from the restaurant, not far from the bay. I thought we might want to be in a public place. But I don't know how long we can stay here before they find us again."

"That's okay, because we have to get to the tower," I said, sitting up. "Just as soon as my head stops pounding."

Darrell gave me a hard look, then stood up, looking toward the water. "Mine is pounding, too. Not because I nearly died but because I forgot to thank my brother for saving my life."

"Oh, sorry," I said. "Thanks."

"Don't mention it," he said. Then he breathed out. "Listen. Does anybody feel weird about Tricia Powell? I mean, I kind of trusted her. Why would she lie about the Chinese symbol of the beacon tower? Lily, can you try to look it up with those magic fingers of yours?"

She smiled. "Of course."

"What would we do without you, Lily?" my dad said as her thumbs flew over the little keyboard on her phone.

"I don't want to say," she said, swiping the screen at whatever results she was getting. "But it probably involves a lot of blank looks."

I sat there, my arms and legs completely wasted, but more and more my brain was starting up again. It winked and snapped at me. Beacon tower. Feng Yi versus Tricia Powell. Who was lying to us?

Then Lily found something. "And this is why I get paid the big bucks. Or I will when I get a job. 'Tower with beacon' or 'beacon tower' is *not* just one character. It's three. See?"

She enlarged the image.

峰火台

Not one of them looked anything like the symbol inside the spice box.

"Mr. Feng really studied the symbol," said Becca. "I watched his eyes, the way he traced it in the air in front of him. So he was trying to deceive us?"

"We don't know that," my dad said softly, almost tentatively, as if he might not believe what he'd just said. "He rescued us twice. Why would he lie if he's a Guardian?"

"Is there some way he could not be dead?" Darrell asked.

"But how could he not be?" I said. "I let him fall."

"You didn't *let* him fall," my dad said, correcting me.

"Dead or not," said Lily, "I think Feng Yi knew exactly what it meant. Maybe he told us 'tower with beacon' to throw us off? He didn't want us to keep going, remember. He said we were involved in something too big for us."

"Wolff said that, too," I said, remembering the Honolulu airport.

"Let's not get ahead of ourselves," my dad said. "One thing is certain. If Mr. Feng turns out *not* to be a Guardian, and if he's still alive, he might now know something we don't. The real meaning of the symbol."

"Which I stupidly showed him," said Becca.

"Not at all," Dad reassured her. "Showing him the symbol has just told us that he may not be someone to trust."

"We do still have the poem," said Becca. "Luckily, I didn't give that away. Wade, you have the translation in your notebook. Maybe we should read it again."

A group of men in dark jackets suddenly walked by. We all froze for a moment, thinking they were more of Wolff's men coming to finish the job. But they kept on walking. One of them told a joke. The others laughed, and they trotted past. Right. Other people were still leading normal lives, having regular conversations, going out for dinner. Sometimes you forget that.

My dad got to his feet and slung the black satchel over his shoulder. "You know, I'm not sure sitting out in the open is the best idea after all. Wade, are you okay to walk?"

"Yeah, fine," I said.

"Then let's keep moving," he said, "while we think."

The sky was clear, and stars were visible above the trees in the park, like pinpricks of light against the black. Dad didn't know the city too well, so we wandered a bit before we came to the streets running along San Francisco Bay.

There were large warehouses every few blocks jutting out into the water. You could see (and smell) that most of them were still working warehouses and part of the fishing industry.

"This is a main avenue called the Embarcadero," he said. "Let's follow it north for a bit. Wade, if you can't read the poem . . ."

"I can do it." I took out the notebook and flipped through the pages until I found it.

Scorpio
The deadly claws of scorpion

Lie quiet in jade's green tomb.
Its guardian stands masked of face
And sinister of hand.
Seek him no more, no more
Upon this moving earth.

No one said anything while a crowd of tourists walked past us, chatting loudly; then Darrell cleared his throat. "Well. We get the first two lines, right? The Scorpio relic was in the box. But the rest of it is about who the Guardian is. And I have to say, the last two lines seem like he's dead, which is not good news."

"Maybe." Lily lifted her phone as if she was going to check it, but she didn't. "Let's forget the last two lines for a second. 'Masked of face' sounds like the Guardian has a mask. But you'd notice some guy going around with a mask, and he'd probably be locked up, so maybe it's not a real mask but more like a disguise. And he's sinister and dangerous. Who do we know like that?"

"Who *don't* we know like that?" I said.

"Right, everyone has been sinister so far, including Feng Yi," said Becca.

Darrell stopped suddenly on the sidewalk, and stayed there until we turned back to him. He was grinning. "Uh, no. The poem doesn't say 'sinister'; it says 'sinister of hand.'"

"So he's holding a gun," I said. "Or maybe . . . a throwing star?"

"So maybe the Guardian *is* Mr. Feng," said Lily.

Still grinning, Darrell shook his head. "Not what I meant."

"Good one, Darrell," said Dad, sharing the smile now. "You figured out that part. The poem writer knows that *sinister* comes from Latin, and it means 'left.' The poem means that the Guardian is left-handed."

"Mr. Chen!" said Becca. "His left hand was the one that . . . the one . . . that . . . you know . . . is missing!"

Looking at Becca made me think of the diary. "Wasn't Andreas left-handed? The diary says so, right? Becca, it's in your translation."

Lily reached into Becca's bag and handed her the notebook. Becca opened it and skimmed a few pages. "Here it is. When Andreas is on the island, Hans says, 'His left hand, with which he is most adept, is black.'" She looked at me, and her eyes shone like stars under the streetlight. She knew what I knew: the puzzle pieces—some of them—were starting to fit.

"So," Lily began, "we're saying that there's some kind of tradition, from Andreas on down, for the Guardians, the *true* Guardians of Scorpio, to be left-handed. That it's all left hands from the very beginning of the relic."

"Mr. Feng isn't left-handed," I said. "The way he

tossed throwing stars. The way he reached for me from the pagoda roof."

Darrell stopped again and stared at the ground. "Say that again."

"I said Mr. Feng isn't—"

"Not you," he snapped. "Lily. Say what *you* just said."

She blinked. "I said there's a tradition that the scorpion Guardian has to be left-handed."

"Whoa," said Darrell, hopping in place on the sidewalk as if he couldn't get it out fast enough. "This whole thing just got a little bit nuttier and a whole lot weirder, and you are going to love me even more, if that's even possible, which it probably isn't—"

"Darrell, please," said Dad, unable to keep from smiling.

"Yeah, catch us up already," Becca said impatiently.

Darrell positioned himself under the nearest streetlight as if it were a spotlight. "Maybe it's a slim lead, but there is totally one left-handed guy we're all forgetting about, except that I just remembered him."

"Darrell," Dad said. I could tell from his tone that even he was getting impatient. "Who are you talking about?"

"The cabdriver!" he said. "The snobby driver with the all-wrong Stratocaster!"

CHAPTER TWENTY

Like everyone else's, my mind zoomed back to this morning to the grumpy bearded cabdriver at the airport who'd told us to beat it.

He drove a wrong-sided British car. His guitar was strung for a left-handed player. He *was* left-handed. He had even said so. But . . .

"Isn't that too much of a coincidence?" I said. "The first person we see in San Francisco happens to be the relic Guardian? And you're saying this because he has a lefty guitar? I'm not sure that even counts as a slim lead."

Lily nodded. "More like nonexistent."

"Is it?" Dad stroked his chin slowly. He pulled us away from the spotlight and down by the side of one of the warehouses. It smelled like fish and salt water. "Darrell, say what you were going to."

"Well," he said, "Wade, you keep saying that there are no coincidences, which I agree with. Besides that, it's actually amazingly logical. Mr. Chen sat next to you because he knew you were . . . with me, a Guardian."

"Very funny," I said.

"Fine, but just listen. The Hong Kong Guardian flies to meet the San Fran Guardian, right? The Frombork Protocol means they need to move the relic. So they meet to figure out a plan."

"What about Mr. Feng?" asked Becca. "What's his part in this?"

"Just a minute." Darrell's brain was obviously popping, and he couldn't be sidetracked. "So the Guardian for here is in disguise as he's supposed to be. As a nasty cabbie. 'Its guardian stands masked of face / And sinister of hand.' He's got a beard. And he's nasty as a disguise, so he doesn't have to pick up regular people. Except yesterday he was waiting for Mr. Chen, all disguised and left-handed because he and Mr. Chen have to do the Frombork Protocol. Ta-da!"

Dad frowned as he always does when he's thinking deeply, then he turned. "Let's keep moving." We made our way back to the street and continued north.

I still wasn't sure I bought it. "Darrell, are you saying

the cab driver shows up at the airport every day to pick up a Guardian in case one comes? And he doesn't pick up anyone else? How does he make any money?"

Darrell shrugged, but Lily started nodding. "No, I get it. Maybe he's superrich, so he doesn't have to pick up just anybody. Or maybe he only comes on certain days of the week. There's a certain day that Guardians come or something."

Then I remembered. "Mr. Chen told me that when we woke up it was going to be Sunday. Today. But I don't know . . ."

"Actually, Darrell could be right," Becca said, getting into it now, while Dad just listened carefully. "Let's say the driver is there every Sunday, like clockwork. Clockwork, right? It's all about time. Anyway, the Guardian doesn't show. So the driver takes off, leaving us to take a shuttle. So why doesn't he do his job as a taxi driver? Because *that's not his job.*"

"But your own question," I said to her. "How does Feng Yi fit into this? Why wouldn't *he* get into the cab?"

Darrell jerked his finger in the air. "Because the cabbie *knew* he wasn't a Guardian, sort of proving that Feng Yi is a bad guy. What if we call the cab company or whatever, and find out who that driver is? His left hand is what Mr. Chen's missing one was supposed to shake!"

Becca smiled. "Very poetic, Darrell. But how can we

find him? There must be hundreds of cabdrivers."

"Not with that kind of cab," Dad said. "I haven't seen another—"

"Got it."

Amazing Lily had already looked up a central number for city cabs on her phone, which she handed to my dad.

I knew his brain was clicking fast when he stretched his shoulders, pressed the numbers on the phone, and stared away from us. He was pulling himself together, ready to be sneaky again.

"Hello," he said. "My name is Rrr . . . Ronald Korman. I'm a photographer for—"

"*Best American Cities!*" Lily whispered.

"*Best American Cities*, and I'm here in San Francisco on assignment to take photos for our next edition. I saw a vintage English hackney cab at the airport, and I'd like to track down the driver. . . ."

Darrell nudged me. "Smooth operator."

A woman on the other end spoke.

"Oh, is he?" Dad said. "I see. What else can you tell me?"

After listening for a minute, he said, "I will, thank you." He hung up and gave Lily her phone. "Our guy is definitely an oddball. Most of the drivers dislike him, you never see him except on Sundays—"

"I knew it," said Lily.

"—and even then he won't pick you up. About the only real thing she could tell me was that his writing name is Papa Dean."

"Writing name?" asked Becca.

Dad chuckled. "He's known as the cabdriver poet. No last name. No phone number. Then she said that he lives 'off the grid' somewhere in Sausalito."

"Which means what?" asked Darrell. "Little Sausage?"

"No," said Dad.

"Where's Sausalito?" asked Lily, raising her phone.

"It's across the bay, on the other side of the Golden Gate Bridge." My dad pointed far up the street. "It's famous for its . . . houseboats."

"Houseboats . . . ," I said slowly. I locked eyes with Dad. "'Seek him no more, no more / Upon this moving earth.' Papa Dean doesn't live on this moving earth. He lives on the water."

"In a houseboat in Sausalito," my dad said.

"Yes!" said Darrell. "I did it!"

"You?" As usual, Lily had leaped upon the information and already had a satellite map of the houseboats on her phone. "There are hundreds, maybe thousands, of houseboats. And if he's off the grid we have no way . . ."

She stopped, studying her screen. "Bec . . . what do you see here?"

"Where?" Becca asked.

"Here!" said Lily, tracing her finger on the screen. "Look!"

"What is it?" asked Darrell.

Becca laughed. "I *knew* Tricia Powell was telling us the truth!"

"All right, spill already," I said. "What are we seeing here?"

"The symbol we found in the spice box," Lily said, bringing up the image we had shown Feng Yi.

"It was never a Chinese character," said Becca, "though *someone* wanted us to think it was. Instead, it's *a map*."

"Of what?" asked Darrell.

"Of this." Lily wiped the screen away from the

symbol to a very grainy satellite image of one section of the Sausalito houseboat docks.

"Holy cow!" said Darrell.

"I bet the dot in the symbol points to the houseboat," Becca said. "That's where we'll find Papa Dean, the Guardian of the Scorpio relic!"

Dad half smiled. "You guys, this is good. Very good. Sara would be proud of how we're piecing all this together. But there's a problem. Feng Yi saw the symbol, too. He may have realized that the symbol is a map, and if, somehow, he didn't die in his fall, he may already be on his way to Papa Dean's. If he lied to us about the map, he's not a Guardian." He adjusted Wolff's black satchel on his shoulder and scanned the traffic. "I have the feeling we're the last people to get this clue. Wade, draw the symbol in the notebook—"

"Let me trace it!" said Darrell, which he did, after placing a page of the notebook over the phone's screen.

"Now Lily, erase the symbol and the satellite map," Dad added.

"Erase . . . ," she said, puzzled at first; then she nodded. "You're right. You're right. We don't need anyone else getting it."

"We need to find that houseboat as soon as possible," said Becca, starting down the street. "And this time, let's get a *real* cab!"

CHAPTER TWENTY-ONE

As we waved at oncoming cabs, I thought: *We're doing it again. We're putting it together. Re-creating the past. Making connections, just like we did in Berlin and Rome and Guam.* Everything we'd figured out since we got to San Francisco was because we'd unpuzzled the puzzles together.

The murder of Uncle Henry might have forced us to start the journey, but we were moving on our own now, and it was an awesome thing.

What was not awesome was the taxi situation on the Embarcadero at night. On our long trudge up the street, we hailed every cab we saw. None of them stopped, not even when Lily jumped up and down on the sidewalk.

"Come on!" she groaned. "We're more important!"

"Can you find a cab service, Lily?" asked Dad. "We'll just have one meet us up the street."

She found one and called. Even then, we had to wait almost a half hour. By the time we tumbled into the taxi, the stars sparkled, the moon was high in the sky, and it was nearly eleven p.m.

"The bridge," said Darrell, "to Little Saus . . . to Sausalito."

"You got it." The driver, an older woman, chuckled in a voice like gravel rolling around a metal pie plate.

When the cab started moving, I felt we were finally getting somewhere. Maybe it was that—or maybe it was when the investigator suddenly called Dad from Brazil, saying that Sara was "nearby, so keep the phone close"—but when we nearly cried with relief, our stomachs cried, too. After the good news, we realized we were starving.

Dad asked the driver to pause for a few minutes so we could grab some takeout at a place called Fisherman's Wharf—a famous area of restaurants and stores—before the drive across the bridge to Sausalito. No problem, she said, pulling over at the first opportunity. She even recommended a place.

Lily, Becca, and Darrell stayed in the car, while my dad and I stocked up on—what else—Chinese food at a cool restaurant overlooking the water that was just closing up for the night.

But when we got back outside, the cab was gone. Darrell stood alone a few feet from where it had been, his eyes wide, his body tense.

I slowed. "What's going on? Where are Becca and Lily?"

Darrell nodded toward the overhang of a nearby warehouse that had been converted to a game arcade. Music jangled loudly from inside. There, in a rainbow of lights around the door, stood Markus Wolff, dwarfing both Becca and Lily, who stood in front of him.

I plainly saw a gun pointed at Lily's side, while Wolff held Becca firmly by her wounded arm. Her brown hair was soaked and clinging to her shoulders; her face was tight with fear.

Dad thrust the food bags at me and took a step toward the overhang, but Markus Wolff gripped his pistol more tightly.

"Do not move another inch," he said.

Dad stopped.

"How did you find us?" I asked sharply, but my voice was hoarse and weak. I caught Becca's glance. Her eyes were wet. She was shaking.

"A surprising question after our discussion about computing power in Honolulu," he said. "Dr. Kaplan, kindly give me the object belonging to Mr. Chen."

Darrell drew up next to us. "The tile? It's at the museum—"

"Not the tile. The tile was merely an entry object into the search for the scorpion. I want the final object. I want his hand."

"His . . . ," I started.

A breath of impatience from Wolff. "The hand Feng Yi stole from Mr. Chen after he murdered him on the plane."

"*He* murdered Mr. Chen?" I asked.

"Please, the hand. It is, I imagine, in the black satchel you have hanging over your shoulder. Mr. Feng's bag."

My dad glanced at the strap, then slid the bag off his shoulder and held it out to the German. "This is Feng Yi's bag? He said it was yours."

"He lies."

"So Mr. Feng is . . . alive?" I asked.

"For the moment," Wolff said. He pushed Lily toward us. "Take the bag," he said. Her hands trembled as she took it from my dad. "Now," he said, "open every compartment."

"I can't. One has a computer lock," she replied in barely a whisper. "Which I guess you don't know, since it's not your bag."

"Ah . . ." Wolff removed his hand from Becca. Dad went for her and Lily, and Wolff let him pull the girls back to us.

"You will wait," Wolff said. He snapped a picture of the lock with his phone. We heard the whoop that the phone made. Some two or three quiet minutes passed, the crazy arcade lights blinking on all of us but the music now off. None of us moved; none of us spoke a word; no one passed by. Then his phone lit up. He studied the image on its screen, closed it, then tapped several numbers into the combination lock. I heard a small click, and the bag opened.

What had he called them? The Copernicus servers? The computing power that put NASA to shame.

Wolff removed something from inside the bag, and my stomach twisted.

Wrapped in heavy cloth was the prosthetic hand of Dominic Chen.

Its thumb and fingers were nearly extended. Its slightly concave palm was open, as if waiting to hold something in it.

It was obviously not real. It was mechanical, but with something nearly alive about it.

His gun still out and trained on us, Markus Wolff examined the hand carefully as he turned it over and over. It seemed less like a hand than an intricate piece of machinery, made of aluminum and wires.

"Well, then, we are done," Wolff said finally, inserting the hand back into the satchel. "It is not essential that I remove you here and now, so I will not. But pray our paths do not cross again in San Francisco."

He bowed his head slightly as he slung the bag over his shoulder, his gun now deep in his coat pocket. "And thank you for your other information, too." He turned his back on us, and, as he had done before on the street outside the hotel, he seemed to vanish into the crowd of tourists.

"What other information?" said Becca. "We didn't give him—"

"No, stop, no!" Lily cried, staring at her phone. "Look! Look!"

As we watched, every photo Lily had taken at the museum—of the spice box, the poem inside its lid, and everything else—evaporated from the screen, and her phone died.

"Start it again," Dad said.

She pressed the On button over and over. Nothing. No image appeared, no icons, no home screen. The phone was wiped clean.

"The servers!" I said. "Wolff said the Teutonic Order had incredible computing power. They probably have spyware, satellites, all kinds of tech stuff trained on us and our cell phones. He knew we called the cab. He knew where we stopped for food. Now he has all of our clues. He knows everything we know!"

Dad growled under his breath. "Give me your phones," he said agitatedly. "We can always buy more if we need them. We know where we have to go, who we have to see tonight. Our flight to New York is at ten tomorrow morning. We know that, and we don't need phones anymore."

"What about the investigator?" Darrell said, handing him his phone.

Dad jammed his eyes shut, then opened them. "Right. I'll keep mine. I'll just take out the battery until later. Lily, please."

"But Uncle Roald, how will we . . . ," she started, but she trailed off, giving her brand-new phone to him. "Okay. I get it."

Dad removed the batteries from both phones, then dumped them into a trash bin. "We're going off the grid. We're just ourselves now, together every second from here on. Understood? No separating."

"But what are we going to do?" said Becca. Her voice was hoarse as she looked across the water at the end of the bridge. "Feng Yi and Markus Wolff know about the houseboat. They know what we know."

"Not both of them, not everything," Dad said. His

forehead creased like it does when he works out a math problem. "They only have everything if they're working together, but they're obviously not."

"That's right," I said. "We showed Feng Yi the symbol. He might guess where Papa Dean's houseboat is, but Lily erased the image of the symbol before Wolff could steal it from her phone."

"And Wolff has Mr. Chen's hand, but Feng Yi doesn't," said Becca. "Wolff said it was the last piece of the puzzle. Guys, we're still in the game."

The lights were going out around us. Fisherman's Wharf was thinning out. It was near midnight now, and cold wind was blowing off the water.

"Here's another thing," my dad said. "I don't know much about prosthetic limbs, but even in the little glimpse I had, I'm pretty certain the synthetic material covering the machinery of Mr. Chen's hand included fingerprints—"

"Ooh, I know why!" said Lily. "To unlock a room or a safe, like Tricia Powell did at the museum! That's what Leathercoat meant when he said the hand was for the last part of the relic hunt."

"Exactly right," my dad said. "We still don't know where the relic is, but I don't think they do, either. Let's get over to Papa Dean's place as soon as we can."

"We can still take a cab to Sausalito, right?" said

Becca, shivering in the wind. "If we use cash, no one can track us."

"Absolutely," said Dad, heading quickly for the street. "Let's go."

So it was settled.

We were off the grid and on the move.

CHAPTER TWENTY-TWO

Because the Wharf was shutting down and cabs were scarce, Lily came up with the idea of going to a nearby hotel to grab a cab from there.

"Where to?" the driver said as we climbed in.

"Sausalito," said Becca.

"And where in Sausalito?" he asked.

"Do you have a map?" Darrell asked. "We'll show you."

"Yeah . . . somewhere . . ." The driver rummaged around under his seat and then passed a wad of crinkled paper over to us.

Darrell studied the map under the seat light. "Here. Liberty Dock."

The driver flipped on his meter. "Now you're talking."

The cab whizzed up to the bridge, crossed it, and wound down through the streets on the far side. A few minutes later, it slowed and pulled into a mostly empty parking lot. "This is as close as I can get. You'll have to walk the rest of the way."

The cab left us there. It was quiet down by the water. The air was so cold my lungs hurt. The sky beyond the bridge was dead black, and the stars seemed on fire.

Where mathematics and magic become one.

Becca shivered again, and I wanted to huddle with her to get warm, but we had no time for anything like that. We saw the sign for Liberty Dock, a long pier that ran straight out from the parking lot. We hurried to it.

"My tracing will tell us which houseboat," said Darrell. "Wade, your notebook, please."

Following his artwork, we trotted down the stairs and slipped through an arch to a floating boardwalk that ran the length of the docks.

"I just thought of something," said Lily. "If Papa Dean has no power in his house, the electronic fingerprints of Mr. Chen's hand don't work on anything there. So whatever it opens has to be somewhere else."

"Good point," Dad said. "If we're right, Papa Dean knows where." He checked his watch. "It's nearly twelve thirty already. I hope he's awake. . . ."

I think we all hoped he was awake. And alive.

If, as Markus Wolff told us, Feng Yi *had* survived his fall from the pagoda, and if he'd figured out that the symbol was actually a map, he could already have found Papa Dean and be long gone. Or he could still be there. "Dad, Feng Yi could . . ."

"I know. Be on your guard," he said. "Everyone."

We made our way quietly down to the end, where the dock made the right angle of the upside-down L. The dot on Darrell's tracing showed the inside corner, but there were two houseboats there. One was marked 47; the other one had no number visible.

"It's the red one on the left," said Becca, studying the tracing.

Darrell squinted. "You know that because I'm such a good artist?"

"I know it because the other house has a light on, but the red one is dark. No electricity. Off the grid."

The plank was short. We stepped down it as quietly as we could. We listened for a minute. Two minutes. No sound from inside. I knocked once on the solid wooden door. The pressure of the knock sent the door swinging open into darkness.

CHAPTER TWENTY-THREE

"**M**r. Dean?" Dad whispered. "Papa Dean?"

No answer. It was cold inside the floating house. Dad didn't want to use the flashlight app on his phone, so the room was pitch-black.

"Hold on," Darrell whispered. He crossed the room with short, careful steps until he came to a wall. He felt around with his hands and found a table. "I thought so. A candle." He moved his hands over on the tabletop. A second later there was a scratch, and a flame lit in his fingers. He lighted two candles.

The orange glow pushed into the room, which was messy, as if there'd been a struggle. Papers were scattered all over the place.

"Uh-oh," said Lily. "This is not a good sign."

"Mr. Dean?" I said. Again, no answer. The front room was small. Taking one of the candles, Becca moved into the small kitchen, then to the bedroom. She let out a soft scream. "Omigod! Get in here!"

We rushed into the bedroom. I nearly threw up.

Papa Dean lay sprawled on the wooden floor, his face twisted in pain, his cheeks and forehead bruised. He was pressing both hands hard on his stomach. Blood pooled under his fingers and on the floorboards beneath him.

Dad was immediately next to him. "Darrell, find someone to call 911."

Darrell ran out onto the dock. I heard him banging on the door of another houseboat.

"Hold on; help will be here soon," my dad said softly.

The grizzled man lifted one of his hands away. In its palm was a bloody throwing star. "You again?" he growled.

"Did Feng Yi do this to you?" I asked.

"Of course he did. You sent him here."

"Sent him? No," my dad said, pressing the wound with towels that Lily brought from the kitchen. "What do you mean?"

"Feng Yi played you *so* well," the man breathed out. "He threw his stars around and you coughed up your secrets to him. The moment he came here demanding the relic, I knew he had fooled you. It was all a decoy: his Star Warriors, his faked death, his oily words, all that was so you'd show him the map to my house. Thanks for nothing."

Darrell was back. "They called for an ambulance."

"You could have helped us at the airport," said Lily.

"I didn't know you," he said. "And I don't like you. I've been fighting the Order for thirty-five years. Then you come in? Don't expect Guardians to like you or help you. This relic cost me everything."

"We're sorry," my dad said. "We got involved because—"

"You don't know enough to be sorry," the man snapped. "You're just a dumb family. This is war."

Which every single person along the way had insisted on telling us. Maybe that was nothing to argue about. We *are* a family, just a family, but I couldn't stop myself.

"You know what, fine. You're right," I said, my chest heaving. "Maybe we shouldn't be Guardians. But we lost someone, too. We lost our mom, and now finding the relics and finding her are the same thing for us."

Ignoring me, Papa Dean grabbed my father by the collar. "He doesn't have the hand, does he? Tell me Feng doesn't have it."

"Markus Wolff has it," my dad said.

We heard sirens. "Then get out," he said. "There's

only one chance now. You don't want to be here. Take the . . . take the . . ." He stretched out a bloody hand to a bookcase by the bed. He tugged a slender paperback from it. Its pages tore as his fingers smeared and fumbled them. He finally seemed to lose all his strength and simply whispered, "Page seven. Get out . . ."

Sirens overlapped other sirens now. They were getting closer. They were almost on top of us now.

"The EMTs will help you," my dad said, taking the bloody book. "I'm sorry for everything. Kids, we have to go!"

CHAPTER TWENTY-FOUR

Lights were coming on in the neighboring house-boats as the sirens wailed to a stop in the parking lot and unloaded their personnel.

My stomach twisted in knots. My throat was thick. I felt like puking from fear. So much blood. So many lies. We *had* sent Feng Yi here. We *were* in the middle of something violent and real and unlike anything we'd ever thought possible. But we had to keep going, didn't we? We had to, to find Sara. We were in too deep to stop.

"The other way," Becca said. "Down the other arm of the dock. We can't let the police find us!"

She was right. The number of times we'd been near a tragedy, an attack, a dead or dying person was far beyond normal. As frightening as it all was, we had to run, even from the good guys.

We got ourselves off the dock into the parking lot away from the ambulances and police cars. We hurried up through the streets winding along the coast. Up toward the vast orange bridge.

If the others were like me, they were beating themselves up. We'd sent Feng Yi right to the houseboat. We'd given Markus Wolff the hand of Mr. Chen. Now both of them were further along than we were.

And closer to the relic.

It also shocked me how much this Guardian hated us. *Just a dumb family.* I tried to work out in my head the connection from Copernicus to the trader Pires to the Chinese court, and on to the theft thirty years ago and where the relics went after that. There were pieces of the puzzle we didn't have, and maybe never would have, but I kept coming back to the way he'd treated us. "Dad," I whispered. "What he said to us. I mean—"

"Not now, Wade. We can't be distracted by that. We still have a job to do." He slowed as we approached the sidewalk, then stopped. "Wait . . ." He choked a little, then just dragged us close to him, all of us, in a bear hug. "Look," he said while we were all pressed against him, "I am either the worst father in the world or a lunatic, bringing you into this, and *keeping* us doing this . . ."

"Neither," said Darrell, wiping his cheeks. "Mom's the reason. She would want us to do this. To keep going. To keep the Order from getting another relic. She's the reason, Dad. Mom is."

My dad was going to say something, but I wouldn't let him. "Darrell's right," I said. "We all know that having a relic will give us more power in this . . . war, if that's what it is. For Sara. But there's the legacy, too. Keeping Copernicus's time machine away from Galina and her murderers is something we have to do."

Lily piped up. "Especially now, right? Both Mr. Chen and Papa Dean have been taken out, and the relic is going to fall into her hands one way or the other. There's nobody left but us. Nobody in this whole city right now. It's only us. Bec?"

Becca's eyes were welling up with tears. She nodded.

I knew Dad was swallowing back tears, too. He loosened his hug.

"You're the best kids ever," he said. "I'm sorry. The clues. We need to read the book. Find whatever is there."

He pulled the bloodied paperback out of his jacket, and we started walking to the bridge again. The cold wind off the water was sweeping up the coast and fluttering the book's cover open.

Becca took it from him and turned the pages. "It's a collection of poems by Papa Dean," she said. "I think it's called beat poetry. The one on page seven is short."

We paused under the streetlamp, listening as she read.

> *Prime Time for D*
> *D is for daybreak and ding-dong.*
> *D is for double and deadline.*
> *D is for duomo, dagoba, and dewal.*
> *D is for doomsday.*
> *D is for digits.*
> *D is for D, as in MDXIV.*

She read it again, and a third time as we started up and across the bridge's pedestrian path. She said, "Anyone want to take a stab at it?"

Darrell grumbled. "Don't look at me. My brain doesn't work that way. It goes in flashes. I can't put things together. I jump at stuff."

"Sometimes a flash is what we need, bro," I said.

"Well, 'double' means Andreas, right?" said Lily. "Hans Novak wrote in the diary that Andreas looked so much like Nicolaus that he could be his double."

"And digits are fingers," said Dad. "For Mr. Chen's hand, maybe. And MDXIV are Roman numerals for . . ." He worked it out in his head. "The year 1514, when Andreas joined Nicolaus. The poem seems to be about the legacy, without actually naming it."

"Deadline could mean that there's a deadline to this whole thing," I said. "The Frombork Protocol, maybe. Or the change of days Ptolemy talked about."

"What about the churches?" Darrell said.

We stopped. "What churches?" Lily asked.

"Well, maybe not *church* churches, but duomo and dagoba and dewal are different kinds of places of worship in other countries. My mom worked on a manuscript about world religions."

"Brilliant, Darrell," said Lily.

My father suddenly seemed to get something. "Becca, may I?" She gave him the book, and he stood under one of the bridge lights and studied the poem. "Places of worship . . . churches . . . 'D is for ding-dong and daybreak.' Churches and church bells? Maybe we're supposed to be looking for a church. A church with a safe, perhaps?"

"The diary! Hans mentions church bells twice." Becca pulled her notebook out of her bag and flipped it open to the new translations she had done in the museum. She read out two passages.

> . . . *the night as black as the pit wherein we discovered Ptolemy's device. In Frombork at this moment, so you*

will understand the hour, we would hear the vesper
bells ring from the cathedral across from Nicolaus's
tower. . . .

"In my mind, Hans," says Nicolaus, "the cathedral
bells toll with every splash of the oar that takes my
poor brother from me."

In a few more hours the sky over San Francisco would be starting to brighten, but right now the night over the Pacific was as black as when Andreas rowed away from his brother. Despite all the evidence telling me it wasn't five hundred years ago, every time we put our heads together we were re-creating scenes from the life of Copernicus.

"Vespers are the bells they ring at night?" I asked.

"Yes," said Becca. "In English novels there are always bells at different times of the day."

"The poem mentions daybreak," I said. "What are those called?"

Lily grumbled. "If I still had a phone, I could look it all up."

"Dad, the phone," said Darrell. "We can call the investigator, too."

Dad looked to the sky above the bridge like he

expected someone up there to tell him what to do. "Okay. A few minutes, that's all." He removed his phone from his pocket and inserted the battery. Seconds later, it lit up. "All right, Lily. Church hours."

"Church hours," she repeated as she called up the browser and keyed in the question, while Darrell paced back and forth, staring at the phone. Lily's search didn't take long. "They're called canonical hours, and there are eight of them: matins, lauds, prime, terce—"

"That's it!" I said. "When is prime? What hour?"

"—sext, none, vespers, and compline," Lily finished. "Prime is at six a.m. Thank you." She passed the phone back to my father.

"Dad, call her," said Darrell. "Call the investigator. Please."

"I am," he said, tapping in the number. "Got her voice mail. It's not quite morning there. Phone tag. Hello. This is Roald Kaplan. My phone is on again. Please call back."

Relieved that Dad had made the call, Darrell started rocking on his feet under the streetlight. "Okay, okay, 'Prime Time for D.' Six in the morning. But there's something else. I can't put my finger on it. . . ." He stopped. "Becca, the brochure. The museum brochure. You still have it?"

"Of course." She fished in her bag and pulled it out. "But why?"

"Wade, your notebook," he said. I grabbed it from my bag and gave it to him.

We watched as Darrell turned the brochure to the page with the picture of Alan Hughes and his wife. He flashed it in front of us. "Alan Hughes died in 1988 after donating the spice box to the museum. That's like three years after the jade scorpions were stolen from the Forbidden City. Who has a pen?"

"Darrell, what are you thinking?" said Dad, slipping a ballpoint from his jacket pocket and clicking it.

Darrell took the pen and started scratching on the brochure.

"What are you doing? I collect those!" Becca yelped.

"Don't you scribble up my notebook!" I said.

Darrell flipped the brochure around. "Look at this picture of Alan Hughes. Who does he suddenly look like?"

Alan Hughes had a big Santa beard scrawled on his face.

"The Wolverine," said Lily.

"The Wolver—" Darrell practically jumped at her. "How do you know about the Wolverine?"

"Dude, I go to the movies," she said calmly. "And you draw him really badly."

"Come on, Darrell," Dad said. "What are you getting at?"

"It's Papa Dean!" he screamed. "Papa Dean is Alan Hughes thirty years later! Sorry about the brochure, Bec, but look at him!"

It was true. He'd nailed it. The face was the same. The features, the eyes. Alan Hughes, the man who donated the scorpion's spice box to the museum as a clue for Guardians, was himself Scorpio's Guardian.

"But what does that mean now?" asked Lily. "Even if they are the same person, they're both out of the picture."

"Why do you want my notebook?" I asked, snatching his pen away.

He turned the pages carefully under the bridge light. "Alan Hughes was survived by his wife," he said, tapping the page in my notebook where I'd copied down the museum's label for the spice box. "Dolly."

"Dolly . . . ," Dad repeated. "Short for . . ." He suddenly flicked his eyes up at the sky; then he closed them and started rocking slightly on his feet as Darrell had just done. Becca started to say something, but I quickly raised my finger, and she stopped.

Dad needed the gears to slip into place.

And they did.

"Dolly is short for Dolores," he said softly, turning toward the city, then checking his watch. "Everyone who's familiar with San Francisco knows that the oldest building in San Francisco is a place of worship, a church, and that that church is called Mission Dolores. 'Prime Time for D' is six a.m. at Mission Dolores. We have four hours to get there."

That was it. We'd figured it out. We started walking.

CHAPTER TWENTY-FIVE

Misión San Francisco de Asís, better known as Mission Dolores, stands at the corner of Sixteenth and Dolores Streets.

We arrived there at 5:46 a.m.

We had walked the whole way, across the great bridge, down the deserted streets. It was miles and miles. We were dead on our feet and empty of everything. But even being empty, we needed to be together, not in a cab or anything, just us, walking together. Most of the time we didn't talk, but when we did, we went over what we knew about the relic.

We were way beyond exhausted before we got there. But we got there.

It was nearing dawn, though the sky had hardly

begun to brighten. Just about the time we reached the mission, it had started to sprinkle, and that sprinkle had now become a steady rain. Not to mention that the already-cold air had quickly turned colder. Changeable weather, changing again.

The narrow, squat building Papa Dean's clues had indicated as a resting place for Scorpio was built of white stone. Four chunky columns flanked a pair of studded wooden doors. A gallery ran over the doorway and just under a peaked roof of Spanish tiles that gleamed now in the morning rain. A simple cross stood fixed at the peak.

On a sunny day, the mission might have looked peaceful, even pleasant. In the rain, knowing what we knew, it looked more like a decorated coffin.

We cased out the mission for a few minutes. No one entered while we hid next to a fence across Dolores Street, at least no one we saw.

"We shouldn't have a problem getting inside," Dad told us. "Many churches are open day and night for people who need a quiet place to pray."

That sounded like what we needed just then. I kept realizing that the investigator hadn't called back yet, and a voice in the back of my head told me that might not be a good thing.

"Let's go," Darrell said, his voice nearly gone.

We crossed the street and the grassy median in between the lanes and walked up the red stone steps leading into the church.

Dad was right. The doors were open.

The long, narrow room inside had rows of wooden benches, a peaked ceiling, and a tall, richly decorated altar at the far end. The space smelled of candle wax, damp stone, and scented smoke, even this early in the morning. The smell might also have simply been the odor of the past. The feeling in there—the walls so old, the dimly colored early light, the almost overpowering hush of the room—made me think of the cave in Guam again. We were near a relic now, just as we had been then. And just like the cave had seemed a couple of days ago, we were now in a holy place. I thought of Sara, mostly Sara, but also about Becca and her arm.

It was silent for minute after minute; then there was a noise, and the hairs on my neck bristled.

His chiseled cheekbones and long black hair caught the candlelight. Of course I knew by now that Feng Yi had never died in his fall from the pagoda. That had been part of his big scam to get us to give him time to find the Guardian. But it was still a shock to see him.

"It took me quite a while, putting the clues together," he said softly, raising a pistol into view. "First realizing who Papa Dean was, then having my agents in Shanghai scour their databases for information, all to give me the simple fact of his wife's name. Dolores. The rest was a leap of intellect, which I have become quite good at. You have brought the key? I hope you have brought the key. You, Wade, managed to snag it from me, during my . . . escape."

"No," I said.

"No," Darrell repeated, shifting back and forth on his feet. "No way."

"Alas," Mr. Feng said quietly. "Then you will perish."

"There are five of us," said Dad.

"Five mortals," Feng Yi said, sneering. "A poor showing against my legendary Star Warriors." He hissed, and a dark shape rose soundlessly from the pews to our left. Then another on the right, and another behind us. Twelve in all, the shrouded fighters under Feng's command, each of whom held an array of sparkling stars.

"You will not escape alive, I promise you that," Feng Yi threatened.

"We don't have the key," Dad said. "Wolff has it."

Feng Yi shrugged. "Then it will arrive soon. And we shall see if the fourth jade scorpion holds the true Copernicus relic."

"It's killed so many people," I said. "Andreas Copernicus died because of it. If the legends are true, what makes you think it won't kill you, too?"

Feng Yi waved his gun hand as if swatting a fly. "It is one of the twelve relics of the astrolabe. Its value is beyond your imagining. You should be grateful I am taking it away from you."

"You murdered Mr. Chen and stole his hand," said Lily bitterly. "You tried to kill Papa Dean. You tricked us the whole time. You and your dumb henchmen. You're not superheroes. Just creeps."

Mr. Feng's face stretched slightly into a thin smile. "Vaults can conceal, museums can collect, time can hide, but people? People are the weakest link in any secret. You should have bowed out before coming this far. You are trying to play our deadly game, but you are, alas, merely a father and his little family—"

"Stop saying that!" I shouted. "We got this far, didn't we?"

Feng Yi's smile faded. "You did. So let us go the rest of the way and await Herr Wolff in the treasury behind the altar, where Mr. Chen's hand will be of use."

Why he didn't just do away with us then and there, I didn't know. Did he need us for something?

He gestured behind us with his pistol, and while his warriors remained in the nave, we preceded Feng to a small door directly behind the altarpiece. With a dull thwack, he blew off the handle and pushed the door open. The church's treasury was narrow. Each wall held a number of vault doors, some with electronic lockers, others with combinations.

"This is where the church stores its precious objects," Feng Yi said. "I wonder if they know what exactly they might have here. The hand's 'fingerprints' will show us. . . ." He smiled at one vault. "There."

Mounted on one plain gray metal door, almost at floor level, was a mechanism with five pads in the position of a left hand.

Someone yelled from the church nave. There were several sets of feet running down the aisle and among the pews, followed by the *whump-whump* of shots being fired. Then came a quick string of Chinese words in a voice I knew too well. The words ended with "Galina Krause."

A flurry of movement followed. Then silence.

Feng Yi's eyes widened when Markus Wolff stepped into the vault, the black satchel over his shoulder, his gun pointed at us.

I smelled the stinging odor of gunpowder wafting in with him.

"Markus!" Feng Yi said, throwing on a fake smile and pointing exaggeratedly to the vault. "I have found it for us. You see? The vault that holds the Scorpio relic!"

Leathercoat didn't fall for it.

"I see many things, Feng," Wolff said calmly. "Your

betrayal, for example. You should know that Galina has only contempt for traitors. Your Star Warriors seem to comprehend this. Only two of your holy dozen remain. I suggested they stand by to remove your body."

Wolff raised his pistol; Feng Yi sneered and grabbed Becca roughly. "I will kill her! Kill her, do you understand! Open the vault. Hurry!" When he pushed his pistol barrel into Becca's neck, she winced, and I wondered if he had forced us into the treasury as some kind of leverage. Dad felt me move and held me back, held us all back.

In the quiet moments that followed, Wolff let out a sound between his teeth. His body tensed. For the first time since I'd seen his dead eyes in Honolulu, they seemed to flash with anger. He stared at Becca so intensely as if he intended to bore directly through her. Finally, he unshouldered the black satchel and removed the prosthetic hand. He carefully placed its fingers one by one on the five pads of the safe door, pressing his own on top of them to ensure the connection. We waited while an old clock on the wall of the treasury ticked toward the hour. Time seemed to slow to nothing.

Nothing moved. Nothing sounded. Nothing.

Then the mission bells struck the hour of prime.

One, two, three . . .

The first peals rang through the room, shuddering

the walls and floor. Then came a subtle trembling behind the vault door.

Four, five . . .

"Like clockwork," Feng Yi said, his face gleeful, crazy, half in candlelight, half in shadow, and his pistol firmly at Becca's throat.

We couldn't move.

Six . . .

The door of the safe clicked and swung open.

Glimmering inside, in the faint glow of the treasury candles, was the pale figure of a jade scorpion.

CHAPTER TWENTY-SIX

The scorpion figurine was intricate and exquisite, what I could only imagine was a priceless example of Ming craftsmanship. The scorpion had eight legs, a short, curved tail and stinger, and a pair of razor-like claws.

Though I couldn't touch it, couldn't even get near it, I felt in my fingers and hands the weight that it possessed. The air in the room trembled around us, as it does when exposed to the beauty and mystery of a true relic. The scorpion sat poised on the floor of the safe like a living thing ready to jump.

"Is it the true relic?" Dad asked. "Or a decoy?"

"After five centuries, no clues remain to determine this," Markus Wolff said, admiring the figurine with wide eyes that now had a little life in them. "The piece must be tested in a laboratory, shielded against radium poisoning, and the shell removed. Even if it does not contain the true relic, its markings may lead us to where the relic hides."

While some of us were feeling the magic of the figurine, I could see the anger building up in Darrell. In the way he stood. In his fiery eyes. His inability to keep still. "So," he growled, "after all the stupid searching. The people hurt and killed. It could still be . . . *nothing*?"

"Or it could be the one!" Feng Yi murmured as he removed the scorpion from the vault. He held it to the candle, but the flame flickered and dimmed mysteriously. Even from a few feet away, I saw the jade appear to be on fire from inside, dulling all light in the room, as if it were its own miniature sun. My knees felt weak. Could the real relic be right here with us? Was this the Scorpio relic of Copernicus?

"I have laboratories in China," Feng Yi said, his eyes flashing. "If this figurine holds the true relic, I will begin my own search—"

The bullet from Wolff's pistol whizzed past Becca's face and into Feng's shoulder. The impact whipped him around. Becca screamed, and I leaped to her despite myself and pulled her to us. Her bandage was bloodstained, her arm weak.

Wounded, Feng Yi waved his gun wildly. We all ducked, and he lunged past us into the church, still clutching the scorpion. Wolff turned. There came a second shot, and a third.

We rushed out into the nave.

Feng Yi was writhing on the floor, the bloody scorpion a few feet away, just out of his reach. Wolff trained his pistol on the two Star Warriors now. Then he removed a lead box from his satchel. Slipping on a single, left-handed protective glove, he started toward the scorpion.

I didn't have time to think. I didn't try. I was running on instinct. "Galina Krause is not getting it!" I yelled. "Never! Not after what she's done to Sara. Or to Becca!" I bolted past Wolff.

"Wade!" my dad shouted. "No!"

I snatched the scorpion from the floor, Wolff's gun on me.

"You cannot!" Feng Yi cried. "The poison! The markings—"

Wolff aimed at my chest. "Give it—"

I threw the figurine down.

As in the cave where Vela was found, all the air in the room was sucked away. Even when the scorpion shattered on the sacristy's stone floor, I heard no sound. Even when it was clear there was no iron scorpion inside the figurine, I heard nothing. Staring at the fragments of jade on the floor, I nearly collapsed. There was no relic. It was the fourth decoy.

For a long moment, Wolff stared me down with his dead eyes. Then he turned to Feng's men. "There is nothing here for you now," he said calmly. "Your leader has fallen. Take him away, or die here."

The two men fixed each other with a look. The game had changed, and they'd understood. Without a word, they hoisted Feng Yi limply between them and carried him from the church.

Dad, Becca, Darrell, and Lily stared at me as Wolff slowly collected the remains of the scorpion in the box. He placed the box into the satchel and slung the satchel over his shoulder. Slipping his gun into the side pocket of his long coat, he turned away.

My father cleared his throat. "What about us?"

Wolff turned, his attention riveted on me. "Wade Kaplan, you may have known the scorpion was a decoy or may simply have been lucky. The Order will reassemble it for its clue. Until then, I have other business."

Becca gripped her bloodstained bandage. She was practically sobbing. "You're letting . . . you're letting us go? Why?"

Wolff gazed at her stonily. "Why? The French call it *carte blanche*." His eyes flickered toward my face. "In war, one uses what one can to win, a lesson you are learning for yourselves."

He paused to breathe in the scent of the candle wax and gunpowder, then concluded ominously, "If I need you again, I will find you."

"What about my mom?" Darrell demanded. "Sara Kaplan. Where is she?"

"Of her I know little," Wolff said, "save that she is no longer in South America as you, and your investigator, seem to believe. I'm afraid that's a trail that will remain cold. Until Galina gets what she wants."

"It's not true, you creep!" Darrell shouted. "The detectives are going to find her—"

I stopped Darrell by rushing up to Wolff myself, staring in his face, and whispering to him, "You opened the vault when Feng threatened Becca. Why? What is it about her? I know you don't lie. Tell me!"

Wolff gazed at me, his eyes again as dead as before. Then he took three steps toward the mission door and paused. "These are tiny questions. Ask yourselves but this: Where is the twelfth relic?"

"The twelfth relic!" I said, flashing suddenly on what Galina had said in my dream. "What does that mean?"

"What, indeed," Wolff said. "The answer to that is the answer to everything. Vela, the others, all will come into our possession eventually." He put his hand on the door and pulled it open. It was raining heavily outside. Smiling, he added, "And now you know far too much to live very long."

He walked out of the church as he had walked into it, silently.

For a moment, we were all too stunned to speak.

Then Lily turned to me. "That was . . . Wade, tell me you knew that wasn't the true relic. Tell me! You could have made us radioactive!"

My knees felt like Jell-O. I sat down in a pew. "It had to be a decoy. It didn't match what Hans wrote in the diary. That the scorpion relic had a long tail, not a short one. Only we have the diary, so only we knew that."

"So where's the real Scorpio?" she asked.

Before anyone could say anything, Dad gasped and tugged his phone quickly from his pocket, putting it on speaker. "Yes? Hello?"

"Hello, Dr. Kaplan." The investigator's voice sounded hoarse and tired. "I am sorry not to respond before now. My detectives and I located the house outside Rio, and we have just finished searching it top to bottom. I am sorry, very sorry, to report that we found no trace of Sara Kaplan. . . ."

And my heart crashed through the floor. Darrell began shouting, and the rest was the mumble of words Markus Wolff had predicted.

". . . so promising . . . arrived too late . . . wife must have been moved . . . other location . . . dead end . . . sorry . . . very sorry . . ."

The dark thing we had all kept at bay in the back of our minds had rushed forward and smacked us down.

After all the hope, Sara was more gone than before.

The call ended, and my dad fell in on himself. His face went dark with sadness; he jammed his eyes closed, squeezing tears down his cheeks. Darrell tore away from Becca and Lily, who had tried to put their arms around his shoulders, and lunged at Dad, pounding him on the back until he wrapped his arms around him. It was like my dream in the cave: everyone confused, grieving, weeping.

How long we stayed that way, I can't even tell you.

Five minutes. A half hour. Time stopped while we died inside.

Finally, Dad pulled us all together, his face stone, his eyes wet, his lips quivering. "We'll figure this out; we have to," he said. "Sara is out there, waiting for us to find her. We need to get to the airport. Retrieve Vela and the daggers. Get on our flight. Go to New York. Keep searching. Our flight leaves in three hours. Come on."

That was all anyone could say. We hurried out of the quiet mission, with Lily and me on either side of Becca, supporting her, Darrell stomping behind us, cursing to himself. The rain was harder but strangely warmer now.

The weather in San Francisco changed in the blink of an eye. I got that. But then, everything that had happened so far was all about *change*.

A wreck of old metal had become a time-conquering machine.

A happy little family had been struck by tragedy and was becoming a band of fighters.

Relic hunters.

Guardians.

We were shouldering more pain than we thought we could. We were growing closer to one another as we pushed forward into a dark and dangerous future. We were getting tougher, faster, harder, stronger.

Whether we were better people now than we had been when we'd touched down in San Francisco, I can't say. *Better* is a tough thing to claim. But one thing was certain. As we hurried past Feng Yi's bloody footprints, washing away in the rain, as we pushed on, haunted by the mystery of the Copernicus Legacy and fearing Sara's fate more than ever, we didn't stop running.

And we haven't stopped running.

Even now.

ACKNOWLEDGMENTS

I am indebted to a host of people and places, all of who helped (some without knowing it) in the writing of this book. First of all, thanks to Beth Dunfey, my long-time friend and editor, for her invaluable (and under the gun) help in nursing and nudging this story to its completion. Then there is the unlikely case of Kevin Peters, who drove me all around the San Francisco area before he mentioned that his last name was an Americanization of the Portuguese *Pires*—a name of some significance in the present book, and one which I had already discovered in my research and decided to use. Tomé Pires (not a relation to Kevin, as far as we can tell) is, as are many characters in the Copernicus series, an actual historical figure. Dual shout-outs to my friends at Copperfield's and Kepler's, two awesome Bay-area bookstores that made me feel so welcome so far away from home. Finally, a thanks to the Asian Art Museum of San Francisco for serving as a setting, as well as to the Hotel Vertigo on Sutter Street, known in these pages as the Topaz, a little homage to Alfred Hitchcock, whose cinematic San Francisco swirled around me as I wrote.

Turn the page for a sneak peek
at the next adventure in the
Copernicus Legacy series in

THE COPERNICUS LEGACY:
THE SERPENT'S CURSE . . .

CHAPTER ONE

New York City
March 17
8:56 p.m.

Twelve hidden relics.
One ancient time machine.
A mother, lost.

Seven minutes before the nasty, pumped-up SUV appeared, Wade Kaplan slumped against his seat in the limousine and scowled silently.

None of his weary co-passengers had spoken a word since the airport. They needed to. They needed to talk, and then they needed to act, together, all of them—his

1

father, astrophysicist Dr. Roald Kaplan; his whip-sharp cousin Lily; her seriously awesome friend Becca Moore; and his stepbrother—no, his brother—Darrell.

"Ten minutes, we'll be in Manhattan," the driver said, his eyes constantly scanning the road, the mirrors, the side windows. "There are sandwiches in the side compartments. You must be hungry, no?"

Wade felt someone should respond to the older gentleman who'd met them at the airport, but no one did. They looked at the floor, at their hands, at their reflections in the windows, anywhere but eye to eye. After what seemed like an eternity, when even Wade couldn't make himself answer, the question faded in the air and died.

For the last three days, he and his family had come to grips with a terrifying truth. His stepmother, Sara, had been kidnapped by the vicious agents of the Teutonic Order of Ancient Prussia.

"You can see the skyline coming up," the driver said, as if it were perfectly all right that no one was speaking.

Ever since Wade's uncle Henry had sent a coded message to his father and was then found murdered, Wade and the others had been swept into a hunt for twelve priceless artifacts hidden around the world by the friends of the sixteenth-century astronomer Nicolaus Copernicus—the Guardians.

The relics were originally part of a *machina tempore*—an ancient time machine that Copernicus had discovered, rebuilt, journeyed in, and then disassembled when he realized the evil Teutonic Order was after it.

What did an old time machine have to do with Sara Kaplan?

The mysterious young leader of the present-day Teutonic Knights, Galina Krause, *burned* to possess the twelve Copernicus relics and rebuild his machine. No sooner had the children outwitted the Order and discovered Vela—the blue stone now safely tucked into the breast pocket of Wade's father's tweed jacket—than the news came to them.

Sara had vanished.

Galina's cryptic words in Guam suddenly made sense. Because the Copernicus legend hinted that Vela would lead to the next relic, Sara would be brought to wherever the second relic was likely to be—to serve as the ultimate ransom.

Wade glanced at the dark buildings flashing past. Their windows stared back like sinister eyes. The hope that had sustained his family on their recent layover in San Francisco—that Sara would soon be freed—had proved utterly false.

They were crushed.

Yet if they were crushed, they were also learning that

what didn't kill them might make them stronger—and smarter. Since their quest began, Wade had grown certain that nothing in the world was coincidental. Events and people were connected across time and place in a way he'd never understood before. He also knew that Galina's minions were everywhere. Right now, sitting in that car, he and his family were more determined than ever to discover the next relic, overcome the ruthless Order, and bring Sara home safe.

But they couldn't sulk anymore, they couldn't brood; they had to talk.

Anxious to break the silence, Wade cleared his throat.

Then Lily spoke. "Someone's following us. It looks like a tank."

His father, suddenly alert, twisted in his seat. "A Hummer. Dark gray."

"I see it," the driver said, instantly speeding up. "I'm calling Mr. Ackroyd."

The oversize armored box thundering behind them did indeed look like a military vehicle, weaving swiftly between the cars and gaining ground.

"The stinking Order," Lily said, more than a flutter of fear in her voice.

"Galina knew our plans from San Francisco," Wade said. "She knows every single thing about us."

"Not how much we hate her," said Darrell, his first words in two hours.

That was the other thing. If their global search for the Copernicus relics—Texas to Berlin to Italy to Guam to San Francisco—had made them stronger, it had made them darker, too. For one thing, they were armed. Two dueling daggers, one owned by Copernicus, the other by the explorer Ferdinand Magellan, had come into their hands. Wade was pretty sure they'd never actually use them, but having weapons and being a little more ruthless might be the only way to get Sara back.

"Galina Krause will kill to get Vela," Becca said, gripping Lily's hand as the limo bounced faster up the street. "She doesn't care about hurting people. She wants Vela and the next relic, and the next, until she has them all."

"That's precisely what I'm here to avoid," the driver said, tearing past signs for the Midtown Tunnel. He appeared to accelerate straight for the tunnel, but veered abruptly off the exit. "Sorry about that. We're in escape mode."

Roald sat forward. "But the tunnel's the fastest way, isn't it?"

"No options in tunnels," the driver said. "Can't turn or pass. Never enter a dark room if there's another way."

He powered to the end of the exit ramp, then took a sharp left under the expressway and accelerated onto

Van Dam Street. The back tires let loose for a second, and they drifted through the turn, which, luckily, wasn't crowded. Less than a minute later, they were racing down Greenpoint Boulevard, took a sharp left onto Henry, a zig onto Norman, a zag onto Monitor, then shot past a park onto a street called Driggs.

Why Wade even noticed the street names in the middle of a chase, he didn't know, but observing details had also become a habit over the last days. Clues, he realized, were everywhere, not merely to what was going on now, but to the past and the future as well.

Becca searched out the tinted back window. "Did we lose them?"

"Three cars behind," the driver said. "Hold tight. This will be a little tricky—"

Wade's father braced himself in front of the two girls. *Dad!* Wade wanted to say, but the driver wrenched the wheel sharply to the right, the girls lurched forward, and he himself slid off his seat. The driver might have been hoping that last little maneuver would lose the Hummer. It didn't. The driver sped through the intersection on Union Avenue and swerved left at the final second, sending two slow-moving cars nearly into each other. That also didn't work. The Hummer was on their tail like a stock car slipstreaming the tail of the one before it.

Lily went white with fear. "Why don't they just—"

"Williamsburg Bridge," the driver announced into a receiver that buzzed on the dashboard, as if he were driving a taxi. "Gray Hummer, obscured license. Will try to lose it in lower Manhat—"

They were on the bridge before he finished his sentence. So was the Hummer, closing in fast. Then it flicked out its lights.

Becca cried, "Get down!"

There were two flashes from its front passenger window and two simultaneous explosions, one on either side of the car. The limo's rear tires blew out. The driver punched the brakes, but the car slid sideways across two lanes at high speed, struck the barrier on the water side, and threw the kids hard against one another. Shots thudded into the side panels.

"Omigod!" Lily shrieked. "They're murdering us—"

As the limo careened toward the inner lane, the Hummer roared past and clipped the limo hard, ramming it into the inside wall. The limo spun back across the road, then flew up the concrete road partition. Its undercarriage shrieked as it slid onto the railing and then stopped sharply, pivoting across the barrier and the outside railing like a seesaw.

The driver slammed forward into the exploding air bag. Lily, Becca, Wade, and Roald were thrown to the floor. Darrell bounced to the ceiling and was back down on the seat, clutching his head with both hands.

Then there was silence. A different kind of silence from before. The quiet you hear before the world goes dark.

Looking out the front, Wade saw a field of black water and glittering lights beyond.

The limo was dangling on the bridge railing, inches from plunging into the East River.

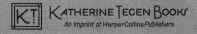

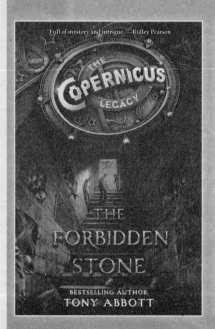
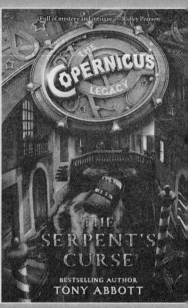

WWW.THECOPERNICUSLEGACY.COM

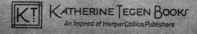

KATHERINE TEGEN BOOKS
An Imprint of HarperCollins Publishers